Davis is an enforcer. His job is to protect the pack in Gillham and the shifters and humans who live there. That's the main reason he agrees to go undercover with the Beasts, the gang threatening everything Davis cares for. The second reason he takes the job is that everyone else on his team has a mate or a significant other, while he's single.

Until he meets his mate.

Calvin is free after spending more than ten years in various labs, but he's not the same man he was before. He's a shifter now, and a bad one at that. No one ever taught him to shift back and forth or to fly in his bat form, and that leads to a lot of problems—like getting tangled in his mate's beard.

Davis and Calvin don't have the time to get to know each other before Davis has to leave. Calvin isn't about to miss out on the chance to be with his mate, though.

Even if it means going after him.

Davis
Copyright © 2020 Catherine Lievens
ISBN: 978-1-4874-2800-6Cover art by Angela Waters

Published by eXtasy Books Inc or
Devine Destinies, an imprint of eXtasy Books Inc

Look for us online at:
www.eXtasybooks.com or www.devinedestinies.com

DAVIS
COUNCIL ENFORCERS BOOK 22

BY

CATHERINE LIEVENS

CHAPTER ONE

Davis wasn't surprised to find out that Devon wasn't Justin's cousin. Those two didn't even look like each other, and if Davis wasn't mistaken, Devon was human, while Justin was a werewolf. He had no idea why Justin had lied to them, but he trusted Justin. He had to. Justin was part of their team now, and that meant they had each other's back. They couldn't do otherwise.

Devon was nervous. There was no ignoring that. He looked like he might bolt at any second, and that wasn't good. Even the slightest noise made him jump. Whatever he'd done, whatever he was running from, was still haunting him. Davis didn't like that. He wanted to help Devon, but he wasn't sure how.

He wasn't the kind of man who comforted people. Usually, people were afraid when they saw him. He was big, *too* big. The fact that he had a full beard and that he towered over most people made him intimidating. No matter how many times he tried telling people that he was just a guy, most of them didn't believe him, especially people who were already terrified, like Devon. Davis wanted to help him, but he wasn't sure Devon wouldn't run away if he came anywhere near him — which was a pity because Davis and his team were supposed to escort Devon to Kameron. The two men needed to talk.

There was also the fact that Lorcan was acting weird. He'd done that ever since they'd first met Devon, and Davis wasn't sure what was happening. Lorcan was his best friend, although he was close to everyone on the team. It was weird that he hadn't talked to Davis about whatever was bothering him, but Davis knew better than to push, especially right now. This was the worst moment to ask for explanations. He wanted to, though.

"Here's what's going to happen," Justin said. He was crouching next to the couch where Devon was sitting with his hands twined together in his lap. "We're going to escort you to Kameron. That means that Nadha will shimmer us to Kameron's house. We'll appear right in front of it, and we'll go in. You'll never be alone, and we're here to protect you. You can trust us. I know it's not going to be as easy as I make it sound, but our job is to keep you safe, and we take it seriously."

Now Davis was even more curious about Devon. But again, this was the worst moment to ask.

Justin was right. His and everyone else's job was to protect Devon. What he'd done or what he was running from didn't matter. He was terrified, though, so Davis steeled himself against whatever was coming. Hopefully, whoever was after Devon hadn't found him yet, but if they had, the team would be ready to face them.

"What if he's found me?" Devon asked, his voice barely louder than a whisper. "What if he's only waiting for this to attack and grab me?"

Justin patted Devon's knee. "I can't promise you he hasn't found you, but I don't think he has. It would have been easy for him to come into the house and take you. You've been here alone several times. So no, I don't think he knows where you are. But he might find out after this. I hope it's something you thought about."

Devon grimaced. "I have, but I also don't have a choice, do I? You won't let me hide in here."

"Because you have vital information for the pack. I know

you're afraid, but I also know you, Devon. You'd never forgive yourself if something happened to the pack and you could have prevented it. You're going to save dozens of lives."

Devon wrinkled his nose. "You don't have to guilt me into this. I've made my decision, and I'm going to stick by it. I was just saying that it's not going to be easy. You're right. I'm terrified. You have no idea what's going to happen if he finds out where I am and what I'm doing. There's no other way out of it, though. I don't want to run for the rest of my life." He looked up, apparently only now remembering that he had an audience. His cheeks pinked, and Lorcan made a strange sound deep in his throat.

Davis frowned and elbowed his friend, then leaned closer. "What are you doing?" he murmured.

He had no idea what was going on with Lorcan, but the sound had been enough to make Devon jump and shrink against the back of the couch.

Lorcan shook his head. "Never mind me."

"Never mind you? Are you serious?"

Sue cleared her throat, getting everyone's attention. "Hello, Devon. I'm Sue, and I'm this team's leader. If you're ready, we should head out. As Justin told you, we won't be exposed. We're just going to shimmer from here to Kameron's house. Once we're there, you'll be safe in pack territory. We'll stick with you for as long as you need us to, and that includes inside the house. I don't know if Kameron wants to talk to you alone, but unless he has explicit orders for that, we'll stay with you even in his office. Is that okay with you?"

Sue was a badass, but she could make herself look soft and gentle. Or maybe she *was* soft and gentle. Davis wasn't sure, but he was scared of her. She was their boss—their leader—and she'd earned that role.

Devon rose from the couch and raked a hand through his

hair. "We might as well go. It's not that I have a choice or like things will change if I wait." He looked around. "How does this work?"

Nadha pushed through the small crowd in Justin's living room and held her hand out. "Take my hand. Everyone else is going to touch me, and I'll shimmer the bunch of us out. Ready?"

Devon nodded, even though he looked less than ready. Davis suspected that if he had a choice, he would have stayed right there on the couch, possibly hidden under a blanket. But instead, he squeezed Nadha's hand and looked around.

Everyone else huddled together. Davis hated shimmering, mostly because having to crowd around a small woman felt awkward. His body took a lot of space, and he hated feeling that way.

But it was over quickly, and he jerked his hand away once he recognized Kameron's house. He relaxed, but not entirely. He looked around, making sure Devon was safe and that no one was waiting to ambush them.

Kameron appeared at the door. "Welcome, Devon. Justin has told me a lot about you."

Devon looked like he wanted to run away. Instead, he rubbed the back of his neck. "I'm sorry I didn't come sooner."

"It's okay. I understand. Why don't you come in? I have coffee and water in my office, and if you're hungry, I'm sure I can find something for you in the kitchen."

To no one's surprise, Devon shook his head. "I'm fine. But sure. Let's go to your office."

He looked behind a few times to make sure the enforcers were following him, and they did. It was going to be a tight fit in the office, but Davis wouldn't have it any other way. This was his job. He'd been told to protect Devon, and that was what he and the others would do. Justin especially was staying close to Devon, and Davis wasn't surprised. He'd taken Devon under his wing, and they'd been sharing a house for several weeks. They were still working on the house, of course, but they were a little family, a family Davis didn't understand. Not that he had to. What happened in Justin's house wasn't his business, even though Justin was a team member.

He wasn't surprised when Justin sat next to Devon on the couch in Kameron's office. He rubbed his back, and Devon's relaxed, albeit not much.

Once they all sat down, Devon looked around. He took a deep breath, briefly closed his eyes, then looked down at his hands. "As you probably know, I'm human. My ex-boyfriend isn't, though. He's a wolf shifter. His name is Elroy, and he wants to destroy the Gillham pack."

Calvin must have been crazy to decide to do this. He'd been trying to show his brother that he wasn't afraid, but in truth, he was *terrified*.

It wasn't even that he was scared of the customers. He knew most of them at least from sight by now, and he knew no one would hurt him. But sometimes, when one of them moved too fast, he cringed. He couldn't help it, not after all the time he'd spent in the labs.

But he was working on it, and he was seeing a therapist. He knew it would take time for the fear to fade away entirely, and that it might never. But he hoped it would. He didn't want to spend the rest of his life living in fear.

So he was dealing with that. He had nightmares and didn't sleep enough, and some days, he wished he didn't have to get up, but he was forcing himself to. He had to show his brother that everything was okay, because Nate would start hovering again if he didn't, and that wasn't something Calvin wanted to deal with.

His brother could be a mother hen when he wanted.

The thought made Calvin smile, but he understood where Nate was coming from. He'd thought Calvin was dead for so long. He'd grieved Calvin. Then he'd found out that Calvin was alive. Maybe not okay, but alive, and he was trying to rebuild his life. But it wasn't easy when Nate refused to let him go anywhere alone. He was afraid he was going to lose Calvin again. Calvin was more than okay not leaving the bar or the apartment above it, though. This was where he felt comfortable, and he wasn't looking forward to exploring Gillham, not yet.

But he wanted to. He always stared out the window, and he watched people walking, going somewhere. They all had a goal, a life they were living, but Calvin didn't. He still thought helping Nate down at the bar was a good idea and that in the end, it would help him become more comfortable with people, but so far, he hadn't seen many results. Of course, it hadn't been very long, so he hoped that with time, things would be different. In the meantime, he'd had to deal with the fear—with feeling powerless and like someone might grab him again at any moment.

And what was worse, he had to deal with the fact that he might shift at any second.

He rubbed his face and looked around. He wasn't a waiter, and that was good. He felt safer behind the bar, and if he did end up shifting, he would create fewer problems. But he *really* hoped he wouldn't shift. He hadn't told Nate that he'd become a shifter yet, and he wasn't looking forward to it.

Rationally, he realized it was stupid. His brother wouldn't kick him out just because he was a shifter. It wasn't like Calvin had chosen to become one. It had been done to him in the labs, and he didn't think it could be changed, not anymore. He'd even asked the doctors, but they hadn't been able to help. So instead of becoming human again, he was now a bat shifter, and he was keeping it a secret from Nate.

It was ridiculous. Nate's mate was a Nix and he had a lot of shifter friends, so he wouldn't care. But he was working so hard on helping Calvin that Calvin didn't want to disappoint him. He wanted to go back to being the man his brother had known before he'd been kidnapped, even though he realized it was impossible. He'd been through too much, and he would never be that man again. But maybe he could become a man who was proud of what he was.

A bat shifter.

Of course, the fact that he couldn't control his shift probably didn't help. He wished he could, but he had no idea how to make that happen, and that made him an easy target. He had to keep Nate safe, and he didn't know how.

"Calvin? Are you okay?" Nate asked.

Calvin jerked, almost dropping the glass he'd been rinsing in the sink. "I'm sorry?"

Nate smiled fondly. "You were in your head."

"I know that. I was thinking."

"You can go back to the apartment if this is too much for you."

Calvin knew Nate wouldn't try to stop him, and he kind of wanted to leave. He wanted to go back to the apartment, where he was safe and he didn't have to face people. But he couldn't. He couldn't disappoint Nate like that, not after everything Nate had done for him, and more importantly, he couldn't disappoint himself.

He hadn't been thinking when he'd decided he wanted to work at the bar, but he knew this was good for him. Most days, he had to force himself to come downstairs, but eventually, he hoped that he would be eager to start working. He wasn't sure what he would do if that never happened.

He was grateful for Nate's presence, though. He made sure that no one tried to talk to Calvin more than they had to, that no one annoyed him or bugged him. Everyone in the bar knew who Calvin was and at least part of what he'd been through by now. They also knew that Nate would pummel them if they as much as looked weird at him. It was both annoying and reassuring.

Nate was much older, and he'd always played big brother. Calvin had grown up knowing that he would defend him against the world. Seeing that in action was weird and overwhelming most of the time, but welcome. Calvin couldn't deny that. He was nowhere near back to normal, and he wasn't sure he'd ever be, but he was also nowhere near feeling comfortable with his new life.

The door opened, and Calvin held his breath. He only released it when he saw Yedley coming through the door.

He missed Yedley. They'd become friends after Yedley had been kidnapped, and they'd escaped together. Yedley hadn't been with the Beasts for long, though. He'd never been in the labs. Even though the experience had changed him, he was nothing like Calvin, and Calvin was grateful for that. He didn't want anyone to have to go through what he'd gone through. Still, he wished Yedley could understand him more, but he was also grateful for his best friend's presence, especially since Yedley had moved out of the apartment Calvin still shared with Nate and his mate.

Calvin couldn't help the wide smile that spread on his face. "What are you doing here? I thought you'd still be scrubbing the floors, or the walls, or something like that."

Yedley grimaced and settled into one of the stools, the one closest to the wall so that he would see if people came toward him. "Don't remind me. I hate that kind of work."

"But you have to do it. That's why you moved in with Justin. I mean, it's your house."

Yedley wrinkled his nose. "Okay, I love the house, but I hate how messy and dirty it is."

"You could have waited to move in." Calvin had hoped

Yedley would, but of course, Yedley had met his mate. Why should he wait to move in with Justin? Calvin might be his friend, but that was all he was. Yedley was moving on, starting a new life, and if Calvin wasn't careful, he'd be left behind.

"I don't want to think about cleaning anymore today. Can I have tea?"

"Of course." Calvin was relaxing just because of Yedley's presence, and he liked it. He realized he was using Yedley like a safe place, though. Eventually, he would have to let go, but he wasn't sure he was ready yet. He didn't think he had to be, either. Yedley, more than anyone else in Calvin's life right now, understood what Calvin had gone through, and he'd been clear when he'd left. He wanted Calvin to feel comfortable with calling him at any time of day or night. He wanted Calvin to know that he would always be welcome in the house Yedley now shared with Justin.

And it helped. It helped to know that he had someone other than Nate, just in case Nate didn't take the fact that Calvin was a shifter well. Nate was so grateful to have Calvin back after all these years that he probably wouldn't even blink if Calvin shifted into a purple cow in front of him. But Calvin couldn't risk it, not yet. Just thinking about telling his brother that he could become a bat made him feel breathless, and he couldn't deal with that right now.

"Justin is probably going to come around with part of his team," Yedley said.

Calvin blinked and forced himself to think about what was happening right now, not about the potential future. "Yeah?"

"They took Devon to see Kameron. I don't know how long it's going to take them, but knowing Justin, he's going to come around once he's done."

"Do you think Devon will come, too?" Calvin had been curious about the reason Devon was on the run ever since Yedley had told him about it. It helped to focus on other people's problems rather than his own, even though he knew it was a shitty thing to do.

"There's no way he's going to leave the house, not unless he's forced to. And I get it. I wish I could do more for him."

"Well, you've done a lot for a lot of people. Give yourself a break. You can't help everyone, especially if they don't *want* to be helped."

Yedley gave Calvin a sharp look. "Are you talking about yourself?"

Calvin shook his head. "I'm going to make your tea."

"Good way to avoid my question."

Calvin flipped Yedley the bird and went to make his tea. Yedley knew what he was talking about, and he'd been pushing for Calvin to speak with his brother ever since he found out that Calvin was a shifter.

But Calvin wasn't ready, and he wasn't sure he ever would be.

"I don't know why you volunteered, but fuck. I wouldn't want to be in your place," Justin said.

Davis rolled his eyes. "That's because you just met your mate. Of course you don't want to infiltrate the Beasts." Being honest with himself, Davis didn't want that, either. But he was one of the few on the team who didn't have a mate or someone waiting for him at home. He didn't have a family that would miss him if he went undercover for months. That was the main reason he'd volunteered. Kameron and Bran had needed someone, and while others would have stepped up if Davis hadn't, he felt better about this than he would have if he hadn't said anything.

So no, he wasn't looking forward to going undercover with the Beasts, but better him than Justin or anyone else on the team.

Justin clapped Davis' shoulder. "Well, thank you."

Davis shrugged. "You don't have to thank me."

"Everyone here does. You took the job so we wouldn't have to."

"As you said, it's a job. I'm part of the team just as much as you are, and I'm okay with volunteering for this."

Justin didn't look convinced, and Davis understood that. He probably could have passed on this job, and Bran and Kameron would have found someone else. There were plenty of enforcers in Gillham who would no doubt have jumped at the chance to do this job. A lot of them wanted to show the council and anyone in charge that they could do this. They wanted glory, but that wasn't why Davis had agreed to do this. Hell, if he could, he'd back right out of it.

But he wouldn't.

He eyed Lorcan as they settled around the table. He was still acting weird, and Davis hadn't missed the way he stuck close to Devon. He'd wondered if that had to do with the job, but he didn't think so. Even Justin, who was one of Devon's only friends, had relaxed after the conversation Devon had with Kameron. Devon was jumpy, which was normal considering he hadn't left Justin's house since he'd arrived there several weeks earlier, and Davis was stunned that he'd agreed to come to the bar. He'd expected they'd have to go straight home, but instead, they were sitting around the table as if they were friends. Devon jumped at every single loud sound, but he really wanted to get his life back into his own hands rather than his ex's, and Davis respected that.

And what an ex he had. Davis knew who Elroy was, just like all the other enforcers. They were fighting against him, even though so far he'd struck through the Beasts. But eventually he would come out, and maybe Devon's presence here would help with that. If Elroy wanted Devon back, he would do something, and the pack would have to be ready for it.

"You shouldn't have volunteered," Lorcan said as Yedley joined them. Davis smiled at him but kept his attention on Lorcan.

Maybe that was one of the reasons he looked so angry. Davis leaned closer to his best friend. "Why not?"

"I could have gone." But as he said that, he looked toward Devon, who was bouncing his knees so hard that his entire body trembled.

"Something tells me that you need to stay here," Davis said. Whatever was going on with Lorcan, it had something to do with Devon, and Davis wanted to give Lorcan a chance with the man, whatever that meant. He knew Lorcan wouldn't hurt Devon. No one here would.

"I don't want you to get hurt," Lorcan said.

"Trust me. I'm not planning on getting hurt. It's not like I'm looking forward to this. I wish I didn't have to go, but who would have gone in my place? You? It's not like we can send one of the girls on the team." Not because they weren't able to do it. Hell, Sue could kick Davis' ass any day of the week without breaking a sweat. But the Beasts weren't only a shifter-only gang. They were also only males, probably because they believed some crap about women being weaker. Davis thought it was ridiculous, but he wasn't surprised. The Beasts were racist, homophobic, and misogynistic.

So that left him, Lorcan, and Justin. Justin was out since he'd just met his mate, and Lorcan, well, Davis might not know what was going on with him, but it was obvious he was interested in Devon, and Davis wanted to give him a chance to see that through.

"What can I do for you?" Nate asked, and all of them looked at him.

They ordered, and Davis leaned back in his chair. He wanted to relax over the next few days. He didn't have to leave right away, but he also couldn't waste too much time.

So he was going to take a few days to go over his things, make sure there was nothing important he needed to do before leaving. And he also had to plan in case he never came back. He didn't want to think about that possibility, of course, but he couldn't ignore it. He might never come back, and he had to make sure everyone knew what to do if that happened.

Lorcan knocked his shoulder against Davis'. "You look like you're going to a funeral."

"I kind of feel like it."

Lorcan frowned. "Are you sure you want to do this? Because Bran and Kameron can find someone else."

"I know. But it's okay. I volunteered. I'll see this through." Davis couldn't help but wonder if he'd done the right thing, and he knew that feeling would get worse once he was with the Beasts. But for now, he knew he had. He was giving Justin a chance to be with his mate, and Lorcan a chance to do whatever he had to do with Devon. He wasn't sure why Lorcan hadn't talked to him, but whatever was happening, Davis hoped it would be resolved by the time he came back.

Because he *would* come back. He had to. He had too much to live for to lose everything.

Maybe it was time to quit the enforcers. It had been a great job for him in the beginning, and it still was. He didn't have a good reason to quit, but with everyone finding their mates, it made him want to settle down. He didn't have a mate to buy a house with or to spend the rest of his life with, but that didn't mean it wouldn't happen. Besides, even if he didn't meet his mate, he could still find a boyfriend or a girlfriend. He could find someone who would care for him, and who he would care for. He wanted that. He loved his team and his job, but it was time for more.

He got up from his chair and stretched. "I'll be right back," he told Lorcan. He tilted his chin toward Devon. "Maybe you should have a conversation."

To his surprise, Lorcan's cheeks pinked. "I don't know what you're talking about."

"Sure you don't. Continue to tell yourself that. But don't think I'm blind. Because I'm not, and I'm pretty sure everyone has noticed the way you're looking at him."

"I'm not looking at him."

Davis didn't push, even though he wanted to. If and when Lorcan felt comfortable talking to him, he would.

But Davis wouldn't be here. He had no idea how long he'd be undercover, but he hoped it wouldn't be any more than a couple of weeks.

He stepped into the hallway that led to the bathroom. He noticed Calvin, Nate's brother, coming out of the breakroom. He smiled at him, but he didn't go anywhere near him. He knew a bit about Calvin's past, and like everyone, he knew how Calvin had come back into Nate's life. The last thing he wanted was to scare him. It was a pity he couldn't get closer, because Calvin was cute. He was Davis' type—shorter than Davis, a lot thinner, with wavy brown hair and big brown eyes. Davis knew he would feel perfect against him in bed. Davis had always had a protective streak, and Calvin's vulnerability called to him. He wanted Calvin to feel safe, though, which was why he didn't go near him.

He stepped into the bathroom and did his business, then washed his hands. He took a moment to breathe, staring at his reflection in the mirror, hoping that he would come out of this in one piece. With the Beasts, anything was possible.

Davis couldn't waste any more time in the bathroom, not without someone coming to see what was going on. He'd made his bed, and now he needed to lie in it. And if he really couldn't do this, if he needed out, he knew that he could always call Bran and tell him he was done. Bran wouldn't protest, and he wouldn't try to force Davis to stay with the Beasts. He would understand and knowing that helped.

Davis stepped out of the bathroom and looked around, sad to see that Calvin was gone. He frowned when he noticed something small flying around the hallway, though. Was it a bird? It wasn't impossible that a bird had come in through a door or window and was now trying to get out, so he stepped closer to the flying little thing. It looked like it wasn't really good at flying, undulating up and down and frantically flapping its wings.

Davis didn't want to grab it, just in case it freaked out, but he didn't know how else to help. He raised his hands, but just then, the thing—a bat—almost dropped to the floor, then turned on itself and flew straight at Davis. Davis lifted his hands to catch it, but somehow, it made it around Davis' hands and flew straight at his face.

Where it tangled in Davis' beard.

Calvin was so mortified that he wanted to *die*.

He tried to extricate himself from the man's beard, but he was stuck, the hair wrapping around his paws and arms.

What the fuck had happened?

Calvin knew the answer to that. What had happened was that he'd shifted without meaning to, just like always. What had happened was that he'd been in the middle of the hallway, and he'd tried to go back into the breakroom, but he hadn't managed before this guy came out of the bathroom. He was desperate to get away. He didn't want to be close to the man, whoever he was—he didn't want to be close to anyone. He was terrified that this guy would tell Nate that he was a shifter, and he didn't know what to do about that. He didn't know how to explain.

He tried to pull away again, but he couldn't break free. Maybe it was time for him to learn how to fly, but how was he supposed to do that when he had no one to teach him? He didn't know how to be a bat shifter. He was pretty sure there were at least a few bat shifters in the pack, but going to them would mean letting people know what he was, and he wasn't ready for that. He wasn't ready for Nate to find out.

It felt like the more he tried to pull free, the more tangled he became in the beard. He pulled and pulled, but he couldn't get free.

Then two large hands cupped him, and he froze.

"Good boy," the man crooned. "Or are you a girl? I don't know how to tell the difference, I'm sorry. Did you come from outside?" The man's voice was soothing. Calvin wasn't sure why, but it made him want to bury himself deeper into the man's soft beard instead of getting free, which was ridiculous.

The man's behavior had helped Calvin calm down, and now he realized that he shouldn't pull on the beard to get free. That wouldn't help. Just like it had before, it would only entangle him deeper into the hair, and that was the last thing both him and this guy wanted.

Calvin forced himself to breathe in and out, and that was when the smell hit him.

It made the world around him tilt sideways. He didn't know what it meant, and he didn't want to think about it right now.

He stayed still while the man gently untangled him, but when Calvin tried to fly away as soon as he was free—and he wasn't sure he could—the man cupped his hands around him again and held him close. Calvin panicked and tried to break out of the hold, but the man didn't let go, and Calvin tangled into his beard again. Instead of getting angry, the man soothed Calvin's fur, stroking his big fingers over it, and even though he didn't know what was happening, Calvin relaxed. The man's hands were gentle, and his touch was everything Calvin had been yearning for even though he hadn't known it.

The man finished untangling his beard from Calvin's claws, then gently lifted him until they could look at each other in the eyes. Calvin blinked and tried to get out of the man's hands, but again, he didn't let go.

Calvin bit him.

It didn't matter how gentle this man was—he needed to get away. He couldn't allow Nate to find out what he was. He couldn't allow Nate to see how much he'd changed. Calvin couldn't be vulnerable, no matter how much he wanted to stay close to the man.

The man yelped and opened his hands, and Calvin flew away. Or at least, he *tried* to fly away. He'd always sucked at flying, and he suspected that was mostly because he hadn't been allowed to. Even now, he wasn't allowing himself to try because he couldn't let anyone find out what he was. That meant that instead of flying to the breakroom like he'd meant to, he flapped his wings a few times, then plummeted to the floor. He hit it fast, and pain exploded in his wings. He prayed nothing was broken, because he needed to get out of here.

Since he couldn't fly, he tried to drag himself toward the door. In the meantime, he was also trying to shift back to his human form, even though it was probably the worst thing he could do right now. This guy, whoever he was, thought that Calvin was a wild bat. Maybe if Calvin allowed him to pick him up him, he would release him outside. That way, the guy wouldn't find out that Calvin was a shifter.

Of course, Calvin had no idea what he'd do if he had to fly around as a bat. He was pretty sure that something would try to eat him, and they would probably succeed.

Warm fingers wrapped around his body again. "Don't bite me again, please. I'm just trying to help you," the man said. His voice was a whisper, and again, Calvin relaxed.

What was it with this guy's voice? With his scent? Calvin should try to run away, but instead, he found himself snuggling into the man's hands, trying to get closer. What was wrong with him? Why was he reacting this way?

The man pulled Calvin closer again. "I promise I'm not trying to hurt you," he murmured. "I just want to get you outside so you can fly home."

Calvin rolled his eyes. As if he could fly anywhere.

The man's eyes widened. "Okay. I'm pretty sure that wild bats aren't supposed to roll their eyes the way you just did. Does that mean you're a shifter, little guy?"

Shit. Calvin was giving himself away, and he couldn't allow that to happen. He didn't want to bite the man again, though, and he held his breath as the man brought him even closer to his face, until their noses almost touched.

The man took a deep breath, and Calvin hadn't thought it possible, but his eyes widened even more.

The man looked so shocked that Calvin expected him to drop him. What the fuck was going on?

"Well, I can't say I expected this to happen," the man said. He stroked a finger down Calvin's back. "And I don't think you expected this to happen, either. Do you think you can shift back? We should probably talk, or at the very least, exchange phone numbers."

Calvin blinked. What was the man talking about?

Calvin decided to try to get away again because this guy didn't seem to be all there in his head. He was gentle enough, but Calvin didn't need to be involved in this, whatever *this* was.

But of course, the man didn't let him go. He wasn't harsh when he kept Calvin in his hands, and that was a relief. But he was also not freeing Calvin, and Calvin wasn't sure what to do about that.

"Don't panic. It's okay. I know it's a surprise, and that's okay. I don't expect anything from you, not right now," the man said.

Calvin wanted to shift to ask him what the fuck he was talking about, but no matter how hard he tried, he couldn't manage. He still had no idea how to control the shifts, which was why he'd been flying in the hallway of his brother's bar as a bat instead of walking around as a human. He needed to get upstairs and lock himself in his bedroom. Nate would understand. He'd think Calvin had been overwhelmed, and he would leave him alone. Hopefully, it would be long enough for Calvin to shift back into his human form.

But first he had to get away from this guy, no matter how nice he smelled.

The man lifted Calvin up again, and this time, he was frowning. "I don't understand. Why are you trying to run away from me?" He paused and smiled, and God, he was so gorgeous. Calvin had always had a type—bigger than him so he could feel protected, rugged but gentle—and that hadn't changed, even though he hadn't let anyone else close since he'd come back. He needed to be protected even more than before, even though it made him feel weak.

"Okay, it's obvious that something is wrong, even though I don't understand what," the man said. He looked around. "Maybe I should find someone who knows who you are?"

Calvin reared back. Was this guy a friend of Nate's? Calvin had thought he'd seen all of them, but then he'd only started coming down to the bar over the past few weeks. Nate had a lot of friends.

And this guy was an enforcer. He wore the uniform, and he wore it well. It made Calvin want to burrow against him, possibly without clothes on, but he couldn't. He needed to shift back, but he had no idea how.

"Okay. Let's do this. I'm going to take you to the bar, okay? We'll find someone who can help, since I obviously can't."

Calvin's heart raced. He tried to fly away again, but he should have known better. He couldn't fly. He'd never been able to.

He tripped out of the man's hands and fell, and he closed his eyes as the floor came closer.

CHAPTER TWO

Davis didn't know what to do. He certainly hadn't ex-pected to meet his mate in the bar hallway. This whole situation was a mess, and he didn't know where to start.

He looked around the hallway. "Okay. I don't know what's happening, or why you're scared, or even why you're not shifting back, but it's obvious you need help. The problem is that I don't know *how* to help you," he told the bat as he crouched to take it in his hands.

The bat blinked. Davis didn't know who it was, but he wished he did. He might be able to help then. Since the bat was in the bar, they might know the owner. Maybe Nate would be able to help. Davis couldn't think of anything else to do, so he moved toward the bar to call Nate.

The bat panicked again and tried to fly out of Davis' hold. Davis tightened his grip, making sure he didn't hurt the bat. "Okay, okay, I'm stopping." He stopped in the middle of the hallway, praying that no one would need the bathroom. He was pretty sure that if someone came by, the bat would panic again, and that was the last thing he needed.

He didn't understand what was happening, but he wanted to help.

He raised the bat to his face again. "So you don't want me to go to the bar. Right?"

The bat nodded. At least this was a way for them to com-municate, even though it made things harder.

Davis licked his lips. "So the bar is out. I *do* think you need a quiet place to spend some time, though. Just nod if you agree with it."

The bat nodded again. Davis wasn't surprised, but he wasn't sure what to do. He didn't think the bat would appreciate it if he took them home to the enforcers building. Besides, that place was not private. Even if Davis managed to get the bat into his bedroom without anyone noticing—and he was pretty sure he could, considering how small his mate was—someone would realize something was happening, and they'd come look.

"My car is in the parking lot," he explained. "How about I take you there? It's close by. You'll be comfortable, and it won't be a place you don't know. We can relax, and you can try to shift. What do you think? Is that okay with you?"

The bat hesitated but finally nodded again. Davis felt a bit better, even though he still didn't like it. He wanted to help his mate. He wanted to give them more than a car. But for now, this was what he had, and he hoped it would be enough.

He left through the back door, hoping his friends wouldn't come looking for him. He didn't think he could explain what was happening without telling them he'd met his mate, and he didn't know if his mate wanted that to happen. He didn't even know if his mate was a woman or a man, dammit. He didn't care, but that was one of the things he should know. He wanted to help, and he didn't know how when he didn't understand what the problem was.

Because there *had* to be a problem. Why wasn't his mate shifting back? Were they stuck in their bat form? Davis had heard of such a thing happening, but that usually meant the labs were involved, and that wasn't the case here. Unless his mate had just escaped from a lab and had somehow managed to sneak into the bar? But that didn't make sense. Why would his mate do that? If Davis escaped from one of the labs, he'd run to his family, or the very least, to the enforcers since he didn't have one. He'd go to his friends, but instead, his mate was here, in a bar.

Davis had a lot of questions and zero answers.

He held his mate close to his chest as he made his way to his car. Once he was inside, he made sure all the windows were closed so that his mate couldn't escape, then he put the little guy—or woman—on the seat next to him and twisted in his own so he could face the bat. "Here you go. I'm worried something is wrong. You don't seem to be wounded, but I'm not a doctor, so I have no idea." Davis reached out and stroked a finger down the bat's back. He wasn't sure it was a good idea because he didn't want to scare his mate even more, but the bat shuddered and didn't try to move away, so he took that as a good thing. "I could call Dallas. He's the doctor for the Gillham pack." He paused. "You know you're in Gillham, right?"

The bat nodded and tried to head toward the window.

"I could take you to the doctor," Davis continued. "Maybe he could help you? Because you're not shifting, and I'm getting worried." Davis reached for his mate, but for whatever reason, that made the bat panic. It tried to fly to the window, but since it was closed, it only ended up smashing against it and falling back to the passenger seat.

The bat squeaked, then tried to fly away again. Davis was pretty sure that if his mate wasn't already hurt, they were going to be soon if they continued like this. Not only weren't they shifting back, but it also looked like they couldn't fly.

Davis gently wrapped his hands around the bat again, ignoring the way its claws dug into his skin and brought it closer to his chest. "There's no need to panic," he murmured. He pressed the bat against his body. "There you go. Just breathe in and out." That usually worked with humans, but he wasn't sure it would do anything in this case. Still, he couldn't think of anything better to do right now. He needed his mate to calm down. He was starting to wonder if the intense panic was maybe the reason why they couldn't shift back, and if that was the case, calming down would help.

He tried to ignore the fact that usually the only people who got stuck while shifting were children. He had no clue how old his mate was, and he prayed they weren't a child. It was impossible because children didn't have mates, but maybe Davis' mate was a teenager? He didn't know, and he wouldn't get answers until his mate shifted.

He stroked his fingertips on the top of the small bat's head. "Just like that. Breathe in and out and calm down your breathing. I promise I won't hurt you. I know you want to fly away, but it's obvious to me that you can't, and I don't want you to get hurt. I'm just going to hold you until you feel better, okay? I'm not taking you anywhere. I promise."

He could feel the bat's heart racing, beating against his fingertips. He wished he could do more, but he was entirely lost, and he didn't like that feeling. He also didn't like the fact that he'd just met his mate, but he was supposed to leave in a few days for an undercover job that would last God knew how long.

This was a mess. The reason Davis had taken the job was that he didn't have anyone waiting for him at home. He didn't have anyone who needed him.

But he did now.

Whatever his mate was going through, whatever the reason they couldn't shift back and that they couldn't fly, Davis suspected they were going to need him in their life. He couldn't back down from his job, though. He couldn't call Kameron and Bran and tell them he'd changed his mind. They would understand if he explained that he'd met his mate, but since his mate didn't seem to want anyone to know about this, he wasn't about to do that. He also wasn't about to get out of this job without an explanation.

How had his life gone from being normal to the mess it was

now? He had a job he didn't want to do and a mate he wanted to stay with but couldn't.

What was he supposed to do? How was he supposed to choose?

Calvin forced himself to obey. He didn't know this guy, but he knew the man was right. He needed to calm down.

He felt like he was having a heart attack. He tried to breathe, but he was still frantic, and he needed something to focus on. Since there was nothing else in the car, no *one* else, he focused on the man who'd found him. The man was still holding him close to his heart, and it helped. Calvin tried to breathe in and out along with him, closing his eyes and forcing himself to relax.

It wasn't easy. If anything, it was one of the hardest things he'd ever done.

Every time he'd shifted before, he'd managed to get back to his bedroom and lock himself in there. Nate knew better than to come in when the door was closed, so Calvin had all the time he needed to relax, calm down, and shift back. He knew that if he relaxed, he'd eventually go back to his human form. That always happened. He wished he could control it, though. He hated feeling vulnerable like this. He knew that this man wouldn't hurt him — and he wasn't sure why he was convinced of that — but it didn't make the situation the best.

But there was nothing else to do, so he focused until he felt better.

Of course, that was when he shifted.

Calvin squeaked and tried to cover himself, even though he knew it was ridiculous. The guy was probably a shifter, so he wouldn't care about nudity. He might care about the fact that Calvin was in his lap, entirely naked and trying to hide both his groin and his face so the guy wouldn't see him blush.

"That's unexpected," the man drawled.

Calvin couldn't leave this car, no matter how much he wanted to. He wasn't about to streak through the parking lot and into the bar. Maybe he should have tried to fly in through the window or something, but that was out now. There was no way he'd be able to shift back to his bat form. Even if he could have, he didn't want to get stuck.

"Now, don't go panicking on me again," the man said. He reached back, and Calvin tensed in his lap. He wasn't sure what the man was doing, but he was relieved when the guy took a jacket from the back seat and gently put it around Calvin's shoulders. It fit Calvin well because the guy was so much bigger than him. It covered all the bits that needed to be covered, and even though Calvin still felt too vulnerable, at least he was covered.

Then the man gently helped Calvin into the passenger seat, and he didn't even try to cop a feel. Instead, he smiled at Calvin and held his hand out. "Calvin. I didn't expect you to be my bat."

Calvin blinked. His hand trembled when he took the man's hand to shake it. "You know me?"

"I'm pretty sure everyone in town knows you. You're Nate's brother. He wants all of us to stay away from you."

Calvin grimaced. "That sounds like Nate. What do you mean with *my bat*?"

Davis blinked. "You don't know?" he asked.

Since Calvin had no idea what he was talking about, he shook his head. He was already surprised that Davis knew him, although he probably shouldn't be, considering Nate. "I have no idea. And you didn't tell me your name."

The man rubbed the back of his neck. "Sorry. I'm Davis."

Calvin smiled. He had never met Davis, but if the man was one of Nate's friends, he was safe.

Still, that didn't solve Calvin's problem. His brain was

stuck on the way Davis said *his bat*, though. "So? What did you mean when you said *your bat*?"

"I don't understand why you can't smell it," Davis said. He wasn't smiling anymore, frowning instead.

"Why don't you tell me?"

Davis looked out the window. "Maybe I should get Nate for you? I'm sure he can help you better than I can since I don't know you."

Calvin clutched the jacket around his shoulders. "Please, no. I don't want you to get Nate. I don't want you to get anyone." He sucked in a breath. He was going to have to give Davis an explanation. "I was human, but I'm not anymore. I was turned into a shifter when I was in those labs."

Davis blinked. "Nate never told me."

Calvin laughed deprecatingly. "That's because *I* never told *him*. He doesn't know I'm a shifter now."

There was a moment of silence, and Calvin prayed Davis wouldn't tell Nate anyway.

He cleared his throat. "The reason I didn't shift back to human earlier is that I can't control my shift. I didn't mean to shift in the first place. I don't know what happened. One moment, I was human, and the next, I was a bat."

Davis rubbed his beard.

Calvin forced himself to look away. That shouldn't be as appealing as it was.

"You have no control over your shift."

It wasn't a question, but Calvin nodded. "I don't. I was never taught to shift. I was never allowed to fly, which is why I can't do that, either." He scowled. "I'm a pretty bad shifter." And it wasn't even his fault.

He'd never wanted to be a shifter. Yes, the thought of being able to become an animal was appealing, but there was an entire set of problems that came with being shifters that Calvin could have done without. While most people accepted shifters now, there was always going to be some people who thought they were barely more than animals. There was also the fact that he shifted without meaning to, and of course, that no one knew about it. He hoped no one in Gillham would get angry at him for not telling them, but especially Nate.

Calvin was in so deep that he didn't know how to climb out.

"At least it makes sense now," Davis said.

"I'm really sorry. I didn't mean to get tangled in your beard or to be rude."

"You weren't rude. I was worried because you weren't shifting, and I thought that taking you to the doctor would help. I'm glad you managed to get back to human form before I did that, though, since it's obvious you didn't want to go."

Calvin rubbed his face. He was tired, but even though he was ready for a nap, he couldn't have that yet. "Please, don't tell Nate."

To Calvin's surprise, Davis reached for him. He gently touched Calvin's fingers where they were keeping the jacket closed around him, then moved his hand away. "I won't tell anyone about this if you don't want me to. Nate might be your brother, but you're an adult. You can make your own decisions, and that includes not telling him about this. I can't say I understand why you don't want him to know, but it's not my business."

Calvin relaxed into the seat. "Thank you. I'm going to have to tell him eventually, but I'm not ready for that."

"And that's entirely understandable, with everything you've been through." Davis cleared his throat. "Well, as I told you, my name is Davis. I'm a bear shifter, and as you can probably see from the uniform, an enforcer. I live here in Gillham. I'm on Justin's team."

Calvin blinked. "You are?"

"I am. I'm surprised you didn't hear about me from

Yedley."

Calvin was, too. Although Yedley didn't exactly talk about Justin's team much. He had mentioned a few of them, but Calvin wouldn't have been able to put faces to the names. "He might have. I just didn't put the two together."

"Of course. Do you want to go back inside? I can help you get to the apartment."

Calvin looked down at himself. "I do need some clothes, don't I? The ones I was wearing are in the breakroom. Nate is going to freak out if he finds my clothes and I'm not nearby."

Davis smiled. "That makes sense. I can go get them for you if you want me to." He hesitated, and Calvin wanted to know what he was thinking. He still hadn't answered Calvin's question about the *my bat* thing, and Calvin couldn't stop thinking about it.

He had a sneaking suspicion he knew what was going on, but he wanted the confirmation. He didn't trust his own nose, even though now it was a shifter's nose. He needed Davis, a more experienced shifter than him, to tell him.

"I'd like that," he said. "But can you first tell me what you meant?"

Davis grimaced. "Are you sure you want to do this now?"

"I'm sure." Calvin wasn't, but that didn't mean he didn't need to know. He needed to find out.

Davis slowly nodded. "All right. What I meant when I said my bat, was that you're my mate."

Davis suspected he should have waited to tell Calvin they were mates, but since he knew how isolated Calvin kept himself, he'd been afraid he wouldn't get another chance, especially with him leaving so soon. He wanted Calvin to know, even though he was shaken.

And Davis understood why. He couldn't imagine being a

human turned into a shifter or the other way around. Calvin had never learned how to be a shifter. He didn't control the shift, and he didn't control flying. That had to be hard on him. Davis could only imagine what it would be like to have the ability to fly and not be able to use it. And what was worse was that Calvin didn't want his brother — the center of his life and his entire family — to know what had happened to him.

Davis didn't know why, and while he wanted to ask, he knew better than to do that. Calvin might be his mate, but they'd just met, and there was nothing to say that he wanted a relationship with him, or even that he just wanted to talk to him.

Davis rubbed his beard. "Obviously, I don't expect anything from you," he said. "I understand that this isn't what you expected and that you're surprised."

Calvin snorted loudly. "A surprise? Hell, yeah. But at least now I understand why I felt the way I felt when you hugged me."

Davis couldn't help but smile. "And how did you feel?" Calvin's cheeks pinked, and Davis wanted to kiss him. He stayed on his side of the car, though.

"You know. I didn't understand what it meant that I wanted to be near you and that I loved your scent. It does make sense now, though, since you said I'm your mate."

"I am. You should be able to feel it."

Calvin wrinkled his nose. "Maybe I am. But I have no idea how it feels. I have no idea what to expect."

Davis tapped his fingertips on the steering wheel. "No one teaches shifters to recognize their mates. It's just something they can do. Think about it. How do you feel when you're near me? How you feel when you can smell me?"

Calvin blushed even harder. "Trust me. You don't want to know," he muttered.

"But I do. I'm not going to hold anything against you,

especially now that I know what happened to you. I can understand why you're distant and why you want some space."

Calvin frowned. "I never said I wanted space."

Davis arched a brow. "Are you saying you don't?"

Calvin shrugged. "It's more that I have no idea what I'm doing. And when I smell you, I feel like I want to be close to you. I feel like I can trust you. I feel like I want you in my life forever." He carefully avoided looking at Davis, and Davis didn't push. The fact that Calvin was already admitting they were mates was a big step, and Davis had to think of Calvin before he thought of himself, especially with what was coming.

Davis cleared his throat. "Like I said, I don't expect anything from you. I might not know your entire story, but I understand. You can take all the time you need to think about it. I won't tell anyone, I promise." Even though he was dying to tell at least Lorcan. He wanted to boast. He wanted to scream from the rooftops that he'd found his mate and that Calvin was the most adorable man he'd ever met.

But he wouldn't. He wanted Calvin to be comfortable with him, and he hated that he was about to leave, even though Bran would no doubt allow him to stay if he explained. He wouldn't be the first one who stayed home after meeting their mate. That was one of the reasons he'd volunteered, after all. Since everyone else had either a mate or a significant other, Davis had felt he was the only one who should make the sacrifice.

But now, he'd met his mate.

It would be easy to get out of it. He wanted to. But he'd given Bran and Kameron his word, and he wasn't going to betray that. He'd made a promise, and he would keep it. Then, he would come back to Calvin, and they would finally be able to get to know each other.

But he had to tell Calvin about this.

"Thank you," Calvin said, his voice just a whisper. "I'm confused. I can't control my shift, I can't fly. I feel like this is something I need to fix before I can even think of being with you. And I need to tell Nate. I'm sure he'll be happy to find out I have a mate, but eventually, he's going to find out I'm a shifter, and I don't know how to deal with that."

Davis wanted to ask why Calvin didn't want Nate to know. He knew Nate pretty well, and he didn't think the man would react badly. He would be sorry, and no doubt surprised since his brother had been human before, but he would accept Calvin. He loved his brother, as much as he loved his mate, and Calvin should know that Nate would never do anything to hurt him. He was the most important thing in the man's life, after all.

"I can give you time," Davis repeated. "I *will* give you time because I have to leave for a mission in a few days."

That got Calvin's attention, and he finally looked at Davis again. "A mission?"

Davis rubbed his uniform. "Yeah, as an enforcer."

"You already told me what you do."

"I just volunteered for a mission."

"That doesn't sound good. Can you give me any details?"

It would probably be better if Davis didn't, but he wanted Calvin to know where he was and what he was doing. He wasn't sure it would matter, but Calvin was his mate. Maybe knowing would help him deal with everything. "You know Devon?"

Calvin cocked his head. "Of course. He's the guy who lives with Yedley and Justin."

"Yes, him. He had a meeting with Kameron today. He told us about his ex-boyfriend and that the man is planning to attack the pack. He's going to use the Beasts."

Calvin reared back, and Davis wanted to hit himself for bringing up the Beasts. They were the ones who'd moved

Calvin from lab to lab and had later kept him prisoner along with the other people they'd kidnapped and had been planning to sell to the labs.

"As I was saying, I volunteered for a mission. Kameron thinks that someone needs to infiltrate the Beasts to keep an eye on them, and since I'm the only one without a mate or significant other, I volunteered."

"But you have a mate."

Dammit. "I do. But I didn't know that until now."

"And you can't get out of this mission?"

Davis wanted to. He wanted to spend time with Calvin. He wanted to stay by his side instead of putting himself into danger. "I could."

Calvin wrinkled his nose. "But you're not going to."

"You're right. I might have met you, but it's obvious you're not ready to be with me. And I don't expect you to. I told you I knew part of your story because Nate told me. Hell, he told everyone, because he wanted us to stay away from you. He wanted us to give you the space you needed to heal, and I'm sure that hasn't changed. So I know you need space and time, and this might be the perfect way for you to have it. I'm going to go on this mission, and you'll have time to think about this."

"What if you never come back?"

"I will. I'm good at my job."

Calvin didn't look convinced, but he nodded. There wasn't much they could do anyway. Davis rubbed his face. He didn't want to leave, but he had to, and first, he had to make sure Calvin was okay. "How about I walk you to the stairs so you can go to your apartment? Or I could pick up your clothes from downstairs."

"The second one, please. Nate will have a fit if he finds my clothes there. He might think someone attacked me."

"So I'll take you back to the breakroom and make sure no

one walks in on you, okay?"

Calvin nodded. He looked around, then opened the passenger door.

Davis rushed out of the car and walked around it, ready to carry his mate. He stopped before touching Calvin, though. He didn't know if Calvin wanted to be touched, especially now that he was in his human form.

Calvin looked down at his feet and wiggled his toes. "Well, that's going to be uncomfortable."

"I can carry you if you want. I promise I won't touch anything I shouldn't be touching."

To Davis' surprise, that got a smile out of Calvin. "Yes, please." He flushed. "I mean, you can carry me." He sucked in a breath. "And I trust you won't touch anything you shouldn't be touching."

Davis couldn't help but smile back. He had no idea where this would go, but now he had one more reason to come back home alive and in one piece, and he was going to do everything he could to make that happen.

Calvin had to force himself not to tense when Davis leaned down to grab him. Davis was gentle, though, and Calvin relaxed without even meaning to.

Davis wasn't just a guy. He was Calvin's mate, as extraordinary as that sounded. Calvin knew he would need at least a few days to wrap his mind around that, but knowing that Davis wouldn't hurt him helped.

Calvin didn't trust a lot of people in his life. Nate, Pryderi, and of course, Yedley. That was about it. Having another person that he could trust touched Calvin's heart in a way he hadn't expected.

Of course, he didn't know how things would go with Davis, but they were mates, and Calvin hoped they would eventually explore their bond. He didn't know if he was ready for it now, or if he would ever be, but he wanted to give this a try.

But of course, Davis wasn't going to be around for long. He had to leave for this mission, and the thought of him being so far away and in danger terrified Calvin even though they'd just met. He didn't want to lose his chance at being happy. He didn't want to miss his chance at having a mate. And he liked Davis. They might have just met, but instead of freaking out or getting Nate, Davis had done what Calvin had asked him to do. He hadn't pushed for anything Calvin wasn't ready to give, and that gave Calvin hope.

He snuggled closer to Davis' chest and took a deep breath. This was the first time since he'd been freed that he was this close to a man who wasn't related to him, or who wasn't Yedley. It was a rare treat, and the fact that Davis was his mate made everything more complicated, yet exquisite. Calvin already knew he would miss Davis once he was gone, even though it was kind of ridiculous. But being mates meant that nothing made sense, not like human relationships did. Being mates meant that even if they decided never to see each other again, they would always share a bond.

They got to the back door, and Calvin started to climb out of Davis' arms. He didn't want to, but he could walk barefoot on the floor inside.

The door swung open. Nate burst out, looking around, frantic.

Calvin groaned. Of course his brother had noticed he was gone. That was just his luck.

Nate's gaze stopped on Davis, who was still holding Calvin close. His eyes narrowed, and he took a step forward, his entire body tense. "Calvin? Is Davis bothering you? What has he done to you?"

Calvin blinked. That, he hadn't expected. He turned

toward Davis and gently patted the man's chest. "Why don't you put me down? I have to talk to my brother."

Calvin was relieved that Davis didn't look angry at what Nate was insinuating. He probably understood where Nate was coming from, but that didn't mean Nate had to be rude.

Davis obeyed and put Calvin on his feet. "I'm going back to my friends in the bar. You know where to find me if you need me."

Calvin nodded. He glared at Nate until Nate moved aside to let Davis pass, then he stomped inside, grabbed his brother's arm, and dragged him to the breakroom.

He waited until the door slammed behind them to turn his brother. "What were you thinking? Why were you so rude to Davis?"

"Cal—"

"Don't *Cal* me. Why are you trying to embarrass me? Did you really think he was bothering me, or worse? Because he wasn't. I wouldn't have been in his arms if he had been. And I'm not a weak princess who needs a white knight in shining armor. Besides, even if I were, you wouldn't be that knight. I don't need you to protect me, especially when there's nothing to protect me from."

Calvin glared at his brother, fully expecting Nate to yell back. Instead, Nate's eyes were wide, and he was grinning.

Calvin blinked, his anger already fading. "What?"

Nate's smile widened. "Do you know how long it's been since you were this passionate about anything?" Nate asked.

Cal opened his mouth, wanting to ask questions, wanting to tell his brother what had happened. But instead, he thought about his next words, then asked, "What are you talking about?"

"I get why you've been so scared all the time. I know that you've been through a lot and that you're *still* going through a lot. You have PTSD, and I wish I could do more to help you.

I understand why you keep yourself isolated, and why you don't talk to me about anything. I know you have nightmares. I know you're anxious and overly cautious. I wish I could do something for you. But nothing I've done has helped."

Calvin shook his head. "That's not true. You help me so much."

"Up to a point, yes. But I want to do more. I wanted to fix whatever was wrong with you." Nate frowned. "Not that there's anything wrong with you, not in that sense. But you know what I mean. I wanted to help you get to a point where you were happy, but nothing I did or said worked. I don't know what happened between you and Davis, but this is the first time you've yelled at me since you came back, and I'm happy about it."

Calvin snorted. "You're happy I yelled at you?"

"Yes. Because at that moment, I saw part of the man you were before, that I thought I'd lost forever."

Calvin wasn't sure what to say to that. He didn't think he'd ever go back to being the man he was before, but maybe it wasn't a bad thing. He hadn't expected to react this way to Davis, but Nate was right. He hadn't yelled at him or gone against him on anything except for the job at the bar since he'd come back. Maybe this was a sign of healing. Maybe it was a sign of the fact that Calvin was finally moving on.

He wanted to tell Nate everything. He wanted to tell him he was a shifter, albeit a shifter who couldn't shift on command and who couldn't even use his wings. He wanted to tell his brother everything and have Nate tell him that none of that mattered, but instead, he chickened out and took the easy way out.

He rubbed the back of his neck. "Yeah, well, there's a reason I'm so passionate about Davis. I'm his mate."

Nate's eyes widened even more, and he gaped. Calvin hoped he wouldn't be angry. It wasn't like Calvin had chosen to be Davis' mate, but if he could have, he wouldn't have made a different choice. He didn't know Davis, but from what he'd seen of the man today, he was a good guy, and Calvin wanted to get to know him.

"He says you're his mate," Nate said. "Since when?"

Calvin rolled his eyes. "Well, I'm not sure how it works, but we just found out about half an hour ago. That's why we were outside."

"I'm happy for you."

"You don't *sound* happy," Calvin pointed out.

Nate shook his head. "That's not it. I *am* happy for you. I know what meeting your mate is like, and I want that for you. I want you to be happy, and I know Davis. He will make sure you are, especially if you're mates. But I won't deny that I'm wondering if this is a good thing. I know it makes me over-bearing and that I need to give you space. You're an adult. But you know I've always been overprotective." Nate shrugged. "That hasn't changed. I want you to be safe. I never want you to get hurt, and I can't help but wonder if eventually, Davis isn't going to do just that."

"That would go for any relationship, though. I'm sure you and Pryderi are going to hurt each other eventually. I could have told him to be careful not to hurt you, but I won't. Like you said, you're an adult as much as I am, and you make your own decisions. You decided to be with Pryderi because it's worth it."

"And you've decided to be with Davis?"

"Not yet. We haven't talked about it, not much. There's so much going on in both our lives, and you barged in before we could discuss it, so that's going to have to wait."

Nate looked sheepish. "Sorry about that, by the way. I didn't mean to tear into him the way I did, but I was worried."

Calvin understood that. It was true that Nate could be overbearing sometimes, but Calvin felt good about it. He'd been alone for so long, and he felt so powerless most of the time, that he didn't mind being protected, even if it was by his older brother.

Nate took a step closer to Calvin. "I just want you to be happy, and if Davis makes that happen, then I'm all in. And I want you to know that you can talk to me if you need to. I realize things might be awkward since I'm your big brother and everything, but I'm here."

Calvin felt even more guilty about not being honest with Nate. He still wasn't sure why he felt the need to keep his being a shifter a secret, but he couldn't help it. No matter how many times he tried, he couldn't ignore the feeling that Nate would freak out if he found out. He already thought Calvin was weak. Knowing that Calvin had changed so much, that he was such a shitty shifter, might push him over the edge.

It was ridiculous, but Calvin couldn't help how he felt.

Nate took a step back and looked Calvin up and down. "You said you just met Davis."

Calvin blinked at the change in topic. "I did."

"Then why were you outside naked with him?"

Calvin was *not* going to answer that, if anything because it wasn't Nate's business. So instead, he grinned at his brother, turned around, and headed to the stairs so he could get dressed.

CHAPTER THREE

Davis hated this job. He wanted to go home, but he was stuck. He'd been stuck for more than a week, and he still didn't have anything to show for it.

He was lucky that the council already had someone who'd infiltrated the Beasts. That man had been able to get Davis in, had given him a good story, but even that hadn't been enough for the Beasts to trust Davis. Not that Davis had expected them to. The gang was hard, and for a reason. They hated anyone who wasn't like them, and they didn't have a problem hurting those people. They didn't see anything wrong with that, and spending any length of time with any member of the gang made Davis' skin crawl. He wanted to go home and shower, get the feeling off his body, but he couldn't.

He was there to stay, unfortunately.

He hated it. He couldn't stop thinking about Calvin, about what he was doing and whether or not he was okay. Davis wanted more than the conversation they'd had, so much more, and he couldn't get it from where he was. He hoped that at least this time away was helping Calvin.

Davis had been stunned when he'd realized that Calvin hadn't told his brother he was a shifter. He didn't understand why. Nate was a bit rough around the edges, but that didn't mean he didn't care for his brother. Anyone with eyes could see that Nate loved Calvin, and Davis doubted that anything would change that.

He wasn't the one in that situation, though. He might know Nate, but he hadn't seen him in a more intimate situation like

Calvin had. Maybe Calvin was right, and Nate wouldn't be able to accept that his brother was a shifter. Davis didn't know, but he did know that he wanted to be there for Calvin when Calvin finally told Nate, and he couldn't because he was stuck here.

He rubbed his face. He needed to stop thinking about home. He couldn't go back yet, so it was useless. The only thing it was doing was hurting him.

"Something wrong?" someone asked from Davis' side.

Davis set his expression, then looked at the man. He was a wolf shifter, and he was just as bad as all the other Beasts. "What's it to you?"

The man raised his hands. "Nothing. You just weren't looking too hot."

Davis arched a brow. "You think I'm hot?"

The man flushed. "That's not what I said, asshole."

Davis didn't want to do this, but he knew the other Beasts were looking at him. Technically, he wasn't a member of the gang yet. He was a prospect, and he was working to become a Beast. He needed to do his best to make sure that happened, no matter how much he hated it.

He got up from the derelict couch he'd been sitting on and stretched himself to his full height. "You were saying?"

The wolf shifter was big, but not as big as Davis. He looked Davis up and down, then took a step back. "Nothing. You're one of those fags?"

Davis should say no, but he didn't want to lose that part of himself. He'd already had to give up most of his personality to be here. At least telling the others that he was gay would help with the ladies he'd been pushing away since he'd arrived. He knew at least a few gang members were wondering why he hadn't yet had sex with any of them.

He crossed his arms over his chest. "Again, what's it to you? Because you're not my type."

The wolf shifter grimaced—Davis should probably remember his name, but the Beasts didn't go by regular names. Every member decided their own name once they became part of the gang, and most of them were ridiculous. This guy was probably called Wolf Fang, or Bloody Wolf, or something stupid like that. It wasn't worth learning.

"As long as you stay away from me, none. I don't care."

That was better than what Davis had expected. "Like I said, you're not my type. I'm not going to come after your ass, don't worry."

"I can't believe you like ass," another gang member said.

"Why? You've never fucked woman in the ass?" Davis asked.

That got him a few titters from the audience in the room.

He was hanging out with the Beasts. That was his main job right now. He'd already done a few drug runs, and of course, he'd made sure the council knew about it. The Beasts didn't trust him yet, though, so they weren't telling him anything important, and they weren't having him *do* anything important, either. For now, they were getting to know him, poking at him like the wolf shifter had just done. It was more than okay with Davis. He didn't want to have to do anything illegal just because they wanted him to. He would if he had to, but he hoped it wouldn't come to that. He didn't want to compromise who he was for a job.

He flopped back onto the couch. "I don't see why you care who I like to fuck," he drawled.

The second gang member—Davis was pretty sure he called himself Tiger—shrugged. "I don't. Means more ladies for me, doesn't it?"

Everyone laughed again, and Davis forced himself to relax, or at least, to appear more relaxed. He doubted he would ever be relaxed when he was with the gang. "Exactly. I'm sure you've noticed I haven't touched any of the ladies."

"I was starting to wonder why. This makes sense."

Davis frowned. "You have something against guys like me?"

"Against gays?" Tiger looked around, then shook his head. "No. One of the guys we work with is gay." He snickered. "Of course, his boyfriend ran away, but that doesn't change what he is."

Davis' heart started racing in his chest, and he had to work not to show his interest. "Yeah? Why did the guy run away?"

Tiger shrugged again. "No clue. It's not like I've ever talked to the guy."

Davis didn't think he was going to get anything more out of that. He was surprised at what he'd already gotten, to be honest. Tiger had just confirmed that Elroy worked with the gang and that Devon had been with him. He hadn't mentioned names, but Davis didn't think there was another man out there who had run away from a guy who worked with the Beasts.

Devon had been telling the truth. Davis hadn't doubted him, but he knew how people's minds worked. They tended to hide things they weren't proud of, and this wasn't something to be proud of. He wasn't sure how Devon had ended up with Elroy, but he was glad the man wasn't with him anymore.

"Look, as long as you keep your mouth shut and don't have anything to say about the people I fuck, I don't care."

The wolf shifter scoffed. "You're not going to fuck a guy in front of everyone, are you?"

"Fuck, no. You might like an audience, but I don't." Mostly because Davis wasn't planning to fuck anyone, so he was relieved that these people wouldn't kick him out. Being gay gave him a good excuse not to go with the prostitutes that came around every night. Maybe now that the guys knew he was gay, they would stop staring at him so much to see if he rejected them.

He rubbed his face again. He was tired, but he couldn't sleep. He hadn't been able to sleep ever since he'd arrived. It had a lot to do with not feeling safe but also with wondering how Calvin was doing.

Davis wished he could contact his mate. He wanted to hear Calvin's voice, wanted to be near him. Calvin's presence would help get the slime out of Davis' body. Nothing else could, and he couldn't wait to go home.

The problem was that he had no idea how long it was going to take. He might have to quit this job, since he wasn't ready to compromise and take drugs or hurt anyone for the sake of it, but since he was only a prospect, so far, he'd only been asked to run drugs around the city. Nothing more might come out of it.

Or it might. Davis had no way to know and no way to find out.

Calvin shuffled and looked at the group of people around the table. He could do this. He could ask Davis' team for news about him.

He had to.

He couldn't believe he'd let Davis leave without talking to him. He'd wanted to, but he'd been afraid. He still was. He was used to being afraid, though. He couldn't let that rule his life the way he had until now, especially not when it came to his man.

Davis had been so gentle with him. He'd been understanding, and he hadn't pushed. Calvin should have gone out there to find him after their first meeting, but he hadn't. He also hadn't told anyone that Davis was his mate yet, except for Nate. Calvin wasn't sure how to explain why, but luckily, Nate hadn't asked for an explanation.

But it was as if Davis would disappear if Calvin talked about him. Maybe it was because he wasn't here right now, or maybe it was just the way Calvin felt. The *why* didn't matter, though. What did matter was that Calvin was terrified that Davis would never come back and that he would lose everything Davis could bring into his life.

He wanted a mate. He wanted a family. He wanted to finally get over what had been done to him and start a new life. He was forcing himself to push, to work at the bar, to talk to people, but it wasn't enough. He wanted more.

He wanted Davis.

It was ridiculous. Calvin and Davis had barely talked so they didn't know each other, but it felt like they did. Calvin realized it was the bond, and he couldn't help but wonder if it would have been different if he'd still been human. Maybe it would have, or maybe not. He doubted being human would have changed anything. He and Davis were mates, and that was the same for all species.

But not having told anyone they were mates meant that Calvin wasn't getting updates on Davis' mission and how he was doing. He could probably have gone to the pack alpha and asked him, explained what was happening, but first, he wanted to try this. These people were Davis' friends. They were the people who knew him best, the people he spent most of his time with when he worked. They would know, right?

Calvin shuffled and looked at the group again. He could do this. He had to.

He took a step forward, then another, until he left his safe haven behind the bar and found himself in the main area. Customers were talking all around him, and only a few of them noticed he'd left the bar. They didn't say anything, though. No one did. They knew that this wasn't like Calvin, but they didn't ask what was going on, and Calvin was grateful.

He sucked in a breath, then made a beeline for the table.

At first, no one there noticed him standing by their side, and they continued to talk, their heads close. Calvin didn't want to listen in on their conversation, but he couldn't help but wonder if they were talking about Davis. Were they worried? Were they talking about what he was doing?

Davis hadn't gone into details when he'd told Calvin about his mission. Calvin only knew that he'd needed to leave, and even though he wasn't sure what he was doing, he couldn't help but wonder how dangerous it was.

He really should have talked to Davis before he left.

Calvin cleared his throat before he could think better of it because if he did, he would run back behind the bar and hide. "Excuse me?"

That got their attention. Justin's eyes widened when he saw Calvin standing there, but he smiled at him. "Hey, Calvin. What can we do for you?"

Calvin bit his lower lip. "I just wanted to ask about Davis."

Justin blinked, and Calvin could see that several team members were confused. "Davis?"

Since Davis and Calvin hadn't talked, Calvin didn't know if he could tell Davis' team members that they were mates. Maybe Davis would want to hide it. Maybe he wasn't ready for anyone to know. Calvin had no way to know, and he wasn't sure whether or not the team was going to ask him why he was so interested in Davis. He wanted to give them the real answer, but he wasn't sure he could. "Yes. I'm worried about him."

Justin looked around at the rest of his team, that back at Calvin. "You want to sit with us?"

Calvin shook his head. He might need answers, but he didn't think he was ready for more. "If you could tell me how he is, I'd be grateful."

Justin frowned, but he nodded slowly. "I can tell you what

I know. He's managed to infiltrate the Beasts, and so far, he's doing okay. He doesn't have any answers for now, so he needs to stay put."

Calvin felt frozen. "He infiltrated the *Beasts*?" Had Davis told him about that? Calvin wouldn't be surprised if he had and Calvin didn't remember. He'd been so confused and terrified that day.

Justin's frown deepened. "Yes. He was sent to infiltrate the gang, or one of the chapters, anyway. We need answers before the pack and the town are attacked."

Even though Calvin was proud of his mate for doing this, he was also frightened. Davis was with the Beasts. He was with the people who'd hurt Calvin so many times over the years.

The Beasts had nothing to do with the labs, of course. He wasn't even sure they'd been a gang when they'd kidnapped him. But over the years as he'd been moved from lab to lab, they'd been the ones to move him. They'd been the ones to close him in a cage, to insult him and laugh at him, at his pain. He hated all of them, and even though it was probably a horrible thing to feel, he wanted them to suffer and pay for what they'd done to him.

And now his mate was in their hands. He'd put himself in danger on purpose to help the town and Calvin.

What was Calvin supposed to do? He didn't know where to start. He didn't know *what* he could do. He was just a guy, a shifter who didn't know how to shift, a bat who didn't know how to fly.

He forced himself to nod. "Thank you."

He moved to leave, but Justin gently touched his wrist, making him freeze. "I don't know what's going on between you and Davis," Justin started. "But if you want more news, ask one of us, okay? We'll tell you everything we know."

Calvin nodded. He was grateful. But he was also confused

and scared, and he had to do something.

What, though?

Calvin went back to the bar, where Yedley was sitting. Yedley was watching his mate and his friends, and Calvin moved toward him, needing a friend. He should have told Yedley he and Davis were mates, but he hadn't found the right moment. Right now, he doubted he ever would. Was there a right moment to do anything?

"Why aren't you sitting with them?" he asked when he reached Yedley.

Yedley shrugged. "We're not attached at the hip, even though we're mates. He can have some time with his friends."

"But he's right there."

Yedley waved Calvin's words away. "I know. What's going on with you?"

This was it. This was what Calvin could do to help Davis.

He leaned over the bar so no one else would hear him. "You know Davis?"

Yedley frowned. "I do. He's one of Justin's team members."

Calvin nodded. "He's also my mate, and he's on a mission. He infiltrated the Beasts." He took one of Yedley's hands and squeezed. "Please, I need you to shimmer me to him."

Yedley jerked back, pulling his hand away. "Are you crazy? What are you talking about?"

"I need to get to him. Please."

Yedley shook his head. "You can't go to him. I might not know the details about what's going on, and I'm sorry that your mate is in this situation—and we're going to talk about how you hid that from me, by the way—but you can't go. You just said he infiltrated the Beasts. Do you know how dangerous they are? You're going to get both yourself and Davis killed."

Yedley was right.

But Calvin still had to go. He needed to help Davis. He needed to face the people who'd hurt him so much and to make sure his mate was okay.

Maybe he could look at Davis from afar and make sure he was okay. That was possible, right? But Yedley wouldn't shimmer Calvin to Davis. That much was obvious. Calvin needed to find another way to do this, and he wasn't sure how.

He turned around, leaving Yedley in his seat, and headed out of the bar. Yedley called for him, but he didn't turn around. He couldn't.

Instead, he rushed into his bedroom and put a plan together. He would call a Nix, one of those who shimmered people around for money. He'd ask them to shimmer him to Davis, and once he was there, he'd find a way in, wherever Davis was. He needed to do this. He needed to be with Davis. They were mates, and that meant it was them against the world.

He had to be brave. He had to be good enough for Davis.

He just prayed that he wouldn't get them killed. This was a new beginning, and he had to be active. He had to *do* something instead of letting the world manipulate him and decide where he should go.

"Come on. We need to go."

Davis blinked. He was sprawled out on one of the couches, faking watching TV but actually worrying about what was going on. He had passed one of the tests, but he needed to pass so many more, even though he'd stood up to the others and had shown them that no matter who he fucked, it didn't make him unworthy to be a Beast.

The fact that he was an enforcer did, but of course, the Beasts didn't know that.

He straightened. "What's going on?" he asked.

The other prospect waved toward the entrance of the house in which the Beasts lived. "Someone tried to sneak in."

Davis was glad he wasn't in that person's shoes. "You have any details?" he asked, standing and following the guy.

"He's in his animal form, and he snuck in through the ventilation ducts."

At least the guy had tried to be smart. Not smart enough for the Beasts, who expected something like that to happen, but smarter than a lot of people would have been. "What do we need to do?"

The other prospect grinned. "I don't know yet, but it's not going to be pretty."

He didn't have to tell Davis that for Davis to know. Things were never pretty with the Beasts, but when they caught someone trying to sneak in? It was like when someone betrayed them. Things would get bloody, never mind pretty.

He and the other prospect went to the entrance. He wasn't sure whether or not they were going to be sent into the duct to grab this guy. Davis couldn't do that, not even in his shifted form—*especially* in his shifted form, since he was a bear. But he wasn't surprised that the Beast in charge right now wanted him and others to be there for damage control. They would want this guy to suffer, to be humiliated in front of as many people as possible.

He stepped into the entrance, and his heart dropped to his stomach, or at least, it felt like it did. The gang leader's right hand, Snapper—because he liked to snap bones—was holding a tiny bat by one of its wings. The bat was trying to break free, but of course, it couldn't. It was batting its other wing, miserably failing, while the second in command laughed.

Davis tightened his hands into fists. It wasn't Calvin—it couldn't be. No matter how much he was reminded of his mate, he needed to focus on what was happening and forget about Calvin, at least for a moment. Once he was back in his apartment, he could contact the enforcers and ask them to check in on Calvin.

The sooner he got to his apartment, the better it would be.

Snapper raised the small bat. "Look what we found."

There were several snickers, but Davis didn't join. He couldn't look away from the bat.

Snapper brought it closer to his face and grinned. "So, are you going to shift, or should I kill you in your bat form?"

A shudder racked through the bat's little body, and Davis held his breath. He wasn't sure what the right thing to do was in this situation. By shifting, the person might be able to give the Beasts an explanation, but knowing the Beasts the way he did, Davis knew they wouldn't accept it. How could they? This bat shifter had entered their territory without their authorization. That called for death.

He wasn't surprised when the bat started shifting. Snapper dropped it to the floor, and Davis winced at the sound it made. He hoped nothing was broken, and he held his breath as the bat became a man. Then, things got even worse because Calvin was standing in front of him.

Calvin wrapped his arms around himself right away. He looked around, his eyes wide with fear, maybe looking for an escape — or for Davis. Davis wasn't sure. How had Calvin found out where he was? What was he doing here?

"I have to say, this is not what I expected," Snapper drawled. "What are you doing here? Who sent you?"

Calvin shook his head. "No one," he said in a tiny voice.

Davis had to step in. He needed to do something before the Beasts killed Calvin. He couldn't allow that to happen. He didn't even care if he ruined the entire undercover mission. The most important thing right now was Calvin, and that was what Davis would protect.

"You should talk before I tell my men to take care of you,"

Snapper said.

"I swear. No one sent me."

Davis sucked in a breath, then took a step forward. "Cal? What are you doing here?" he asked, making sure to keep his voice steady and calm. Inside, he was frantic, but he couldn't allow the Beasts to see that.

Calvin turned toward him, his wide eyes already filling with tears. "I was looking for you," he said, his voice trembling.

Snapper stepped in, pushing Calvin to the side, almost toppling him to the floor. "You know this guy?"

Davis had to play this the right way. "Yeah, I do. He's my boyfriend."

That surprised Snapper, who blinked. "Your boyfriend?"

Davis crossed his arms over his chest. "Yeah, my boyfriend. You have something against that? Because I already had this conversation earlier today, and no one cared."

Snapper narrowed his eyes. "I don't care who you fuck. What I do care about is how he got here."

"He probably just missed me. I shouldn't have left him behind when I decided to come."

Davis looked at Calvin, who nodded frantically. "He didn't tell me why he was coming here, but I missed him. And I wanted to make sure he was okay."

A few Beasts in the room laughed. It *was* kind of ridiculous. Calvin was short, and as had been obvious when he'd been grabbed, there wasn't much he could do against the Beasts. He couldn't keep Davis safe.

But Davis could keep *him* safe, as much as possible, and that was what he was going to do.

"You heard what he said," he explained. "He missed me, and he came to find me. That's all. He's not a spy."

Snapper looked at Calvin again. "Well, he'd be a damn bad spy if he was one, that's for sure. He can't even fly."

52

"That's because he never intended to do anything. He was looking for me."

"This isn't protocol."

Davis scoffed. "Yeah? Well, I wouldn't be the only one with a significant other here, and that's not even counting all the prostitutes who come around every night. His arrival might be on the weird side, but he's only here to warm my bed, nothing more."

"I say we kick the guy out," one of the Beasts growled.

Davis wasn't surprised. He'd never expected universal support, especially coming from these people. He wasn't one of them. He never would be, even though they didn't know that. But he expected some people to grumble about the fact that he was gay, and the thing that had surprised him was that it hadn't happened yet. It was now, though.

He turned toward the Beast who'd spoken. "What the fuck do you want?"

The man looked at him. He was shorter than Davis but just as broad, and Davis knew he would be a problem. "We don't want you fags in here."

Davis arched a brow. "No? Isn't your boss a fag?" Davis had gleaned that bit of info, but he hadn't been sure it was the truth until now. He hoped it was. It would help him.

The man's expression twisted. "Don't talk about him that way."

"Why not? He fucks boys, like me. So why do you have a problem with me and not with him?"

The man roared and reached for Davis. Davis had expected it, though.

His clothes exploded around him, pieces of jeans and fabric shooting through the air as he shifted into his bear form. He rose on his haunches, exposing his entire height, and growled as he reached for the guy who wasn't coming for him anymore.

Good. No matter how little Davis wanted to spread blood, he would do it if it was needed to keep Calvin safe.

The guy wasn't backing down, not anymore. He shifted, too, and Davis found himself fighting a lion.

Shit. He really could have done without this.

The lion jumped for him, and Davis hit him in the face with a paw. Blood spurted, but it wasn't enough to get the shifter to back down. The lion roared at Davis, then jumped toward him again, and this time, his fangs made contact. They tore through the flesh of Davis' arm, and Davis snarled. It hurt, but it was easy to forget the pain when he focused on Calvin, who'd paled so much that he looked like he was about to faint.

Davis needed to finish this as soon as possible. He needed to take Calvin away from the Beasts.

He grabbed the lion's mane, pulled him off even though it hurt, and threw him against the wall. The lion snarled when he got back to his feet and stepped toward Davis, but thankfully, Snapper finally stepped in.

"Stop it, both of you."

Davis obeyed. He didn't want to, but he knew he had to.

"Shift," Snapper continued.

Davis obeyed again. He stood there, entirely naked and not caring one bit. "He attacked me," he growled.

"I know. I was there."

"He's a fag," the lion shifter said. He had bloody cuts on his face from Davis' claws, and Davis felt smug about them.

"And you fuck *human* whores," Snapper said. "I don't see how it's different."

He looked back at Davis, then at Calvin. He frowned, and Davis prayed he would make the right decision, or at least, the right decision for Calvin. "What are you going to do with him?" he asked Davis.

"He's my boyfriend. I'm going to take him home and make

sure he knows he made a big mistake by coming here. But I won't kill him, and I won't hurt him."

"That's fair. As long as you can keep control over him, you're free to do whatever you want with him. Take him home. I don't want to see either of you for the rest of the day."

Davis was so relieved that his knees felt weak, but he made sure that none of those emotions showed. He couldn't allow them to. He couldn't allow himself to be seen as weak.

He needed to be strong for Calvin.

Calvin could only breathe in and out. His heart raced so fast that it felt like it was about to jump out of his chest, and he was doing his best not to look anyone in the eyes. He wasn't sure what would happen if he did, but he could imagine it wouldn't be good.

The man who'd caught him turned around, leaving him in the middle of the room. Calvin tried to cover himself, but he only had two arms, and he was entirely naked. He hated feeling this exposed and vulnerable, waiting for something bad to happen. There was no way out of it, though, not now. He needed to wait and see what came next.

He should have realized this was a bad idea. Yedley had told him, but he'd decided to go on anyway, and now he knew it was the wrong thing to do.

He'd suspected it when he'd arrived in front of this house. The Nix he'd hired to shimmer him to where Davis was had been worried, and he'd asked Calvin if he was sure he wanted to stay. Calvin hadn't been, but he'd said yes anyway, and he'd thought he was smart when he decided to shift and use the AC ducts to sneak into the house. He'd had a hard time with it, since he didn't control his shift yet, but focusing on Davis had helped, and so had the desperate need to get to him.

It hadn't been. He'd been caught almost right away, and this was the result. Davis was hurt because of him, and he'd put his mate in danger.

A blanket wrapped around Calvin's shoulders, and he jumped, scrambling to get away. He realized the person who'd put the blanket on him was Davis only seconds later, but he still felt like he needed to run. Instead, he breathed in and out, then forced himself to look up at his mate.

Davis' arm was bleeding. Calvin gasped, then reached for Davis, but Davis took a step back and shook his head. "Not here. Not now," he murmured. He grabbed Calvin's hand and pulled him toward the front door. "I'm taking you to my apartment," he said, his voice harder.

Calvin swallowed. He knew Davis would never hurt him. He wasn't that kind of man. Calvin was sure of that, even though they barely knew each other.

But Davis wasn't the same Davis he was in Gillham. Here, he was a Beast. He needed to act like one. The thought was terrifying, and Calvin prayed that would only last until they were out of this place.

He couldn't wait. His skin felt like it was crawling. It was as if everyone was staring at him, but he didn't dare look up to make sure of it. He didn't care. It didn't matter. He needed to get out of here as soon as possible, and nothing else mattered.

He and Davis stepped out of the house, and the gravel of the driveway was harsh on Calvin's feet. He didn't say anything, though.

Davis dragged him toward a line of bikes, and Calvin swallowed. "A bike?" he asked.

That finally got a half-smile out of Davis. "Everyone here uses a bike. It's better than a car. Faster. You don't think you can ride on it?"

Calvin looked down at himself. "Not naked."

Davis stopped and looked around. "Okay. Where did you leave your stuff?"

It took Calvin a second to orient himself. "Back there." He pointed toward the back of the house. "It's where I saw the duct. I'm sorry, Davis."

Davis shook his head. "Don't speak, not yet. Wait for me here. I'll grab your clothes and find something I can wear."

Then he was gone. Calvin sucked in a breath and waited, nervously bouncing his foot. He wanted out of here. He never wanted to come back. He was tempted to beg Davis for both of them to leave. He didn't think Davis would say no, even though he was doing his job.

But could Calvin really do this?

He wasn't sure he wanted to ask Davis to give up his job for him. He'd come here to make sure Davis was okay, but he realized now how stupid he'd been. There was nothing he could do to help Davis. As soon as he'd been found out, he'd cowered. He wasn't an enforcer. He wasn't brave. He was powerless, helpless, and the situation showed that once again.

He wasn't sure what he'd been thinking when he'd decided to come, or maybe, he hadn't been thinking at all. But now, he was here, and he wasn't sure there was a way out of here for now.

"Here you go," Davis said gruffly when he came back. He was holding a bundle of Calvin's clothes, and he handed them to him. He was wearing a pair of jeans and a white t-shirt that was too tight for his frame.

Calvin made quick work of putting his clothes on under the blanket. He wasn't sure what to do with it now, but Davis took, folded it, and gave it back to him. "Are you ready to go?" he asked.

Calvin nodded, even though he wasn't sure. He couldn't stay here, though, and the only way out was on the back of Davis' bike.

Davis climbed onto the bike, and Calvin followed his lead. It had been a while since he'd been on one, but he was grateful for the chance of thinking and not speaking. He leaned his cheek against Davis' back and closed his eyes, letting the feeling of the bike under him take his worries away, even if it was only for a few moments.

Seriously. What had he been thinking? Davis was his mate, and he was in danger. Calvin had acted on instinct. He'd felt like Davis needed him, and he hadn't stopped to think about that. He should have. He hoped he hadn't ruined Davis' job, although he couldn't say he would be sorry if he had. He wanted Davis to come home with him. He didn't want to leave Davis here.

The bike slowed, and Calvin blinked his eyes open. He didn't recognize the place where they arrived, but he didn't like it. The building of apartments was run-down, and there was garbage in front of the entrance. He wasn't surprised when Davis climbed off the bike and dragged him toward it, though.

He *really* wanted to go home.

They both stayed silent until they walked into what Calvin guessed was Davis' apartment. He didn't look around. He opened his mouth to speak, but before he could, Davis grabbed him and pulled him into his arms.

Calvin shuddered. He wrapped his arms around Davis and held him as close as Davis was holding him, finally breathing easier. "I'm sorry. I know you're angry."

Davis shook his head against Calvin's neck. "Not angry. Terrified." He finally stepped away, or at least, he tried to. Calvin didn't let him, though. He didn't want this to end, not yet. He wasn't sure what Davis would do now, if he would send Calvin back to Gillham, if he would decide he didn't want Calvin in his life after all, and Calvin needed to make the best out of this.

Davis cupped both of Calvin's cheeks and tilted his head so they could look at each other in the eyes. "What were you thinking?" he asked, his voice deceptively soft. "I was terrified. I thought I was about to lose you. I thought you were going to be killed in front of me."

Calvin swallowed. "I should have thought better about this. I know I shouldn't have come. I don't know what I was thinking. I was worried about you, and I care about you. I don't want you to get hurt."

Davis' eyes widened, but he nodded. "You're right. You shouldn't have come."

"I'm sorry if I ruined your job."

"I don't care about that. If I could, I would grab you and go home right away. There's a lot hinging on his job, and I can't just leave. I want to, but this is the reality of things. I can send you home, though. You have to promise me you'll never come back here."

Calvin nodded. He had no intention of coming back. He might hate that Davis was here and what he needed to do, but he realized that he would be more of a hinderance than anything if he stuck around.

Davis' shoulders slumped. "Good. I'll call Bran and have someone pick you up." He reached for his jeans, but his phone rang before he could take it out. He and Calvin looked at each other, and Calvin held his breath as Davis took his phone out.

Davis looked at the screen and frowned. He held a finger, silently telling Calvin to keep his mouth shut, and he answered. "Hello?"

Calvin was surprised that he could hear the other side of the conversation, although he shouldn't have been. He was a shifter now, and he had shifter senses.

"Prospect?" a hard voice asked.

"Yeah."

"Bates here."

Davis' eyes widened even more, and he looked at Calvin. "Sir?"

The man chuckled. "You can call me Bates. I heard what happened earlier."

Already? Calvin hadn't expected that.

"I'm sorry for my boyfriend, sir." Davis paused. "Bates. He shouldn't have come, and I told him so."

"I want to meet him."

Calvin took a step back and shook his head. He didn't want to meet this guy, whoever he was. Davis seemed to know him, but Calvin didn't want to.

"I'm not sure that's a good idea."

"I don't know if it is, but I don't care. I want to meet this man who put himself in danger to get to you."

Calvin wouldn't have a choice, would he?

Chapter Four

Davis couldn't say no, no matter how much he wanted to—and he wanted to so much. But Bates was the head of the Beasts. He was the gang leader, and no one could say no to him, especially not a prospect.

Davis looked at Calvin, who looked terrified again. He didn't know what to say. "I'll see you back here in half an hour," Bates said.

Davis opened his mouth to answer, but Bates hung up on him, and he was left looking at his phone, not knowing what to say.

He lowered his arm and looked at Calvin again. "I'm so sorry," he said.

Calvin shook his head. "It's not your fault."

It wasn't Davis' fault, and it wasn't Calvin's, either. "We'll find a way out of this."

"What do you think he wants?" Calvin asked, his voice soft.

Davis had no idea. "Well, Bates heard what happened today. He didn't sound angry, so I think he's wondering why you came. He's probably curious about you."

"I'm not curious about him, though. What am I supposed to do? You can't say no, right?"

"I tried, but you're right. I can't just say no. You can't, either, even though you're not a gang member."

To Davis' surprise, instead of freaking out, Calvin squared his shoulders and stood up straighter. "Okay. Talk to me. Explain to me how I'm supposed to behave, what I'm supposed to say. I need to know before we go."

Davis blinked at his mate. "What?"

Calvin glared. "Look, we both know there's no way out of this. You just said so. That means I need to face this, and while I'm not looking forward to it, I want to make sure I do everything I can to help you and that the both of us make it out alive. So tell me how I should behave."

He was right. Davis needed to prepare him since there was no way out of this. "You only speak when you're addressed directly," he started. He paced the room, glancing up to look at Calvin every so often. "You don't mention Gillham or the pack in any way, shape, or form. I don't know if they would associate me with Gillham if you did, but I'm not going to risk it. We can't allow anyone to find out that I'm undercover."

"I'm not an idiot."

"I never said you were. But I also know how hard it is to be undercover. Trust me, the first thing you're going to want to do is to run away, and the second will be to confess every single thing you did in your life just so you make it out of here alive. You'll even tell Bates about the candy you stole when you were in first grade."

That seemed to get the anger out of Calvin. "I promise I won't say anything about Gillham or the pack. I know it would put us in danger."

Davis stopped in front of him. "It wouldn't just put us in danger. We already *are* in danger. Mentioning either of those things would make it so that we'll both die." Davis paused. He didn't want to say all of this, but Calvin needed to know what he was facing. "They would torture us first, though. They would want to know why we're here, who sent us, what we found out."

Calvin wrapped his arms around himself. "I'll be careful. I want to go home just as much as you do. I won't do anything to put this in jeopardy." Calvin paused. "Anything else?" he said with a grimace.

Davis still couldn't believe Calvin had come here. He wasn't sure he understood why, but now wasn't the moment to ask about it.

He reached for Calvin and grabbed both his mate's arms. "I need you to promise me something," he said.

Calvin's glare was back. "Let me guess. You want me to leave you if anything happens."

"Exactly. I need you to leave me behind. I won't be able to defend myself if I obsess over you and what's happening to you. Do you understand that? I need to know you're safe. And you can shift and fly away if anything happens. I can't do that."

Calvin shook his head. "I can't, either. You know I don't control my shift. No matter how hard I try, I won't be able to shift on command."

Davis gave him a little shake. "You're going to have to try. I need to know that you'll be safe if anything happens to me, if the Beasts find out what I'm doing here. Please."

"I'll do what I can," Calvin finally said.

Davis supposed it was better than nothing. He knew the problems Calvin had with his shift, but this was their best plan — and their only one.

Calvin hesitated, and Davis frowned. His mate had some-thing in mind, and even though he didn't know what it was, he wanted to find out. If Calvin thought of anything that could help them, Davis would take the chance and run with it. They would need everything they could find to make it out of this alive. "What?" he asked when Calvin still didn't speak.

"We could bond."

Davis blinked. Had he heard that right? "What?"

Calvin straightened. "We could bond, just in case we get separated. That way, we'd be able to feel each other's emo-tions. We'd be able to feel if either one of us is in danger or in pain, or whatever."

Davis took a step back and rubbed his face. He was tired, and he wanted to go home. He still could. He could call Bran and have someone shimmer over to grab them. They could leave, and no one would know about it. The Beasts would look for them, but they wouldn't be able to find them.

But the pack wouldn't have an answer. They wouldn't know what the Beasts were planning, which was why Davis was here. This was his job, and it was an important one. He needed to protect Gillham, the pack, but most of all, Calvin.

Calvin and his brother lived in Gillham. If the Beasts arrived, if they attacked Gillham and the pack, they might hurt people Davis cared about, including Calvin. Davis couldn't allow that to happen. He didn't want to. He needed to keep Calvin safe, and to do that, he had to play along, and so did Calvin.

"This isn't how I was planning to bond with you," he said.

Calvin snorted. "It's not what I had in mind, either. I thought it would take me months to get used to your presence in my life. I thought I would fall in love with you before doing this. But this is our best bet to make it out of this alive. I promise I'll do my best to fly away if I can if something happens, but I won't leave you entirely alone. I want to be able to feel what's happening to you if I have to go, and I won't agree to leave otherwise."

Davis huffed, then pulled his t-shirt up and off his head. "All right, let's bond."

Calvin snapped his mouth shut and stared at Davis' chest. "Holy shit," he murmured.

In any other circumstances, Davis would have felt proud of the way his mate was staring at his body. He knew he wasn't everyone's cup of tea. He was too tall, too hairy, too muscled. But Calvin didn't seem to have a problem with anything he was seeing, and it made Davis want to preen a bit.

But they didn't have time.

Davis reached for Calvin, pulling him close until there were wrapped around each other. He tilted his head to the side. "You can bite me," he murmured.

Calvin shuddered in his arms. "I don't know how to do that."

"Close your eyes. Follow your instincts. Smell me. Once you have my scent in your nose, your bat will take over."

Davis closed his eyes and gave Calvin the time he needed. They didn't much, because Bates was already waiting for them, and the sooner they met with him, the sooner they could come home, but they needed to do this the right way. It was already nothing like the situation Davis had imagined, but he couldn't change it. If this helped to keep Calvin safe, then he would do it without hesitation.

Calvin's nose rubbed against the skin of Davis' neck. Davis had to bow down a bit, which was uncomfortable, but he wasn't about to take this anywhere close to the couch or a bed. They didn't have time for sex, no matter how much he wanted to, and he knew that bonding would push them toward that.

But this was business. It couldn't be anything else, not right now.

Something scraped against Davis' neck, and his own fangs punched out in answer. He gently cupped the back of Calvin's neck and tilted his head to the side to give himself easier access, then he bowed down, pressing his lips against Calvin's flesh, letting his mate's scent wrap around him.

It might not be the perfect moment to bond, but it would still bring them together forever, and Calvin would be Davis'. Davis had always wanted this, and now he had it.

Did the circumstances really matter?

Calvin was terrified. There were no two ways around it.

He'd been an idiot. He hadn't been thinking when he'd decided to come here, and now, he possibly had ruined everything Davis had been working for since he'd left Gillham. He didn't know what to do about it, either.

But he could change that. Calvin might not know what to do, and being an enforcer wasn't what he'd expected to do, ever, but he would do everything he could to help Davis. Even though he'd promised Davis that he would run if anything happened, there was no way he was leaving his mate behind.

This was what bonding was about. It would link them together forever, and Calvin would have one more reason to make sure Davis made it out of this alive.

Davis was right. Once Calvin let instinct guide him, his fangs came out of his gums. He almost jerked back in surprise, because it had never happened, not in his human form, but instead, he pressed himself even closer to Davis.

Davis was solid against Calvin. His body was hard, and Calvin wanted to do so much more than just bite him. The thought of sex was petrifying, but it was something Calvin wanted to explore eventually. To make that happen, he had to help Davis out of this situation, though.

He sank his fangs into his mate's neck. He wished they could take this moment, make it just for them, enjoy it, and think only about that, but he knew it wasn't possible. No matter how hard it was, this was business right now. He hoped that eventually, they would find themselves in bed together and that they could bond again. He knew it didn't work like that, but he didn't count this as bonding, not in the sense he intended. It was true they were linking their lives together, but they'd have a lot of time to make it happen in reality. They would have to make this more intimate next time, make sure that no one was trying to kill either of them.

In the meantime, this was good enough.

Davis' blood filled Calvin's mouth, and Calvin closed his eyes. He didn't like the taste of blood, so he drank it down as fast as he could, then took another sip. He had no idea how much blood he needed to drink to bond them, so he continued drinking even as he felt Davis finally bite him, too. It made him shiver, and he wished they were both naked.

He couldn't remember the last time he'd thought about sex, but this was good. He could feel Davis was hard from where his cock pushed against his stomach, and it was all he could do not to reach down between them and grab it. Instead, he smiled when he felt the bond snap into place, then stopped drinking Davis' blood and sealed the wounds with his tongue.

He and Davis looked at each other, taking a moment to enjoy this.

"It's done," Davis said.

"I know. We're bonded."

Davis raked a hand through his hair. "I just wish we could have done this differently."

Calvin decided to be brave for once, and he reached up, kissing Davis' cheek. "It doesn't matter to me how it was done or why. The important thing is that we're bonded, and that it makes both of us safer. Now we should probably go. I'm sure your boss is waiting for us."

Davis grimaced, but he didn't let Calvin go, not yet. "His name is Bates, and you need to remember it. He won't be happy if you don't."

The last thing Calvin wanted was to make the guy happy because he didn't deserve it, but he realized that it would make things easier for him and Davis. "Bates. Right. And he's a shifter, of course."

"All the Beasts are. You're ready?"

Calvin didn't think he'd ever be ready to do this, but he nodded anyway. He took a step back and let Davis take his t-shirt from the floor where he'd dropped it. When Davis moved, Calvin saw the wound on his arm, and he gasped. "You're hurt." He'd forgotten about that.

Davis shook his head. "It's nothing. We need to go."

"Not before I take care of this. At least let me bandage it. Please."

Davis looked exasperated, but he nodded. Calvin made sure to be as fast as he could, even though he wanted to take his time and clean the wounds. Instead, he grabbed some bandages from a box Davis handed him that was full of medical supplies, and quickly wrapped Davis' arm. He would have time to clean it and make sure it wasn't infected as soon as they were back here.

Because they would be. Calvin couldn't allow himself to think differently.

Then they were on the move, on the bike and back to the house they'd just left. Calvin knew it was the place where most gang members lived. He wasn't sure why Davis was allowed to have his own apartment, but he was grateful for it. He wanted to ask questions, but it became harder and harder the closer they came to the house. Calvin tensed so much that he felt like he might break if anyone touched him.

Then Davis parked in front of the house.

Calvin sucked in a breath, even though it felt like he couldn't breathe, and he climbed off the bike. He looked up at the house, and from outside, it looked just like a house anyone would live in. It was huge, but that wasn't unusual when shifters lived together. There were so many packs and prides and other groups who wanted to live as a family unit.

But the Beasts weren't a family unit. They were a gang, and they were dangerous.

"Remember what I told you," Davis murmured as he and Calvin walked toward the house. "Talk only when you're asked. Don't look anyone in the eyes if you can avoid it. Keep your head down. Play shy. Let me speak."

Calvin had no problem with any of that. If anything, he couldn't wait to keep his mouth shut.

They walked in. Calvin had to force himself to breathe. He couldn't freak out, or rather, he could, but he couldn't show the Beasts he was.

The entrance was empty, and Davis took a right, walking down a hallway. Calvin followed him, wishing he could take Davis' hand but not knowing if that was allowed. Probably not. Even if the Beasts didn't kick Davis out right away because he was gay, they probably would frown on any sign of affection between two guys.

Davis stopped in front of a door, looked at Calvin, then knocked.

"Come in," a loud voice called out.

They obeyed. Calvin took small, short breaths, his heart racing, and his stomach feeling like he might throw up. He hoped he wouldn't.

"Bates," Davis said. "You wanted to see us."

Calvin sucked in a breath when he saw Bates wasn't alone. The man he supposed was Bates was sitting behind a desk, but there was another man on the other side of it. The guy didn't seem to care about their presence, though, and it helped Calvin relax, albeit just a tiny bit.

"What happened?" Bates asked.

Davis rubbed the back of his neck. "I already apologized, but I want to do so again. Calvin didn't mean to make a mess. He was just worried about me. He wanted to find me." Davis squeezed Calvin's shoulder. "You know how mates are."

Bates arched a brow. "Mates?"

"Yeah. We're bonded. I probably should have brought him along with me from the beginning, but I wasn't sure how the gang would take me being gay. I know the members aren't always the most accepting."

Bates his lips twisted in amusement, or at least, Calvin thought so. "You're right. So your mate wants to be with you?"

"He does. He's not a danger. He just wants me."

"And he's a shifter."

"A bat shifter, yes."

Calvin could feel Bates' gaze on him, and he had to force himself not to move. He could do this. He could help Davis. He was the reason they were in trouble right now, and he would do whatever it took for them to be safe, and possibly, *hopefully*, for Davis to do his job and be able to tell the pack what the Beasts were planning for Gillham.

Davis expected Bates to kick him out, at the very least. In truth, he thought Bates was going to make sure he could never come back by beating him up and making him disappear. He wouldn't have been surprised if that was what happened. The Beasts didn't look kindly at people who went against them, and even though Davis was one of the prospects, by having Calvin with him and by defending him and fighting with another prospect, he'd put that in jeopardy. He'd gone against the Beasts, and no matter the reason, he would have to pay for it.

He made sure Calvin stayed behind him as they faced Bates, but he should have known that wouldn't last long.

Bates leaned back in his chair, staring. It made Davis want to shuffle, but he forced himself to stay still. He couldn't show even one ounce of weakness, not if he wanted to make it out of this room—not if he wanted *Calvin* to make it out of this room. He prayed that Bates wouldn't try to hurt Calvin. Bates didn't have a conscience, and he led the Beasts with an iron fist. He didn't take disobedience kindly, and Davis knew this wasn't going to be pretty.

"So. Where is that mate you were talking about?" Bates asked.

Davis stepped aside to expose Calvin, even though he didn't want to. He stayed close, his arm wrapped around Calvin's waist, and he was relieved when Calvin leaned against him. "This is Cal."

Bates' eyes narrowed as he took in Calvin. Davis knew he wasn't seeing the same thing he was. When Davis looked at Calvin, he saw a gentle man who'd gone through hell and back, and in some way, who was still there. PTSD wasn't a joke, and he wished he could take that experience away from Calvin. But he knew Calvin probably wouldn't want him to even if he could. What Calvin had been through had made him the man he was now. That included his fears, but also a strength, everything that made him what he was now.

Bates, on the other hand, probably didn't see anything more than a piece of ass, and the thought was enough to make Davis see red.

"You're here for your mate?" Bates asked.

Calvin nodded. Davis was relieved to see he wasn't talking, since he hadn't been asked to, and he started to relax. Maybe the meeting wasn't going to be a disaster after all, although a lot of that was on Bates' shoulders. He was the one in charge, and he was the one who made decisions.

"You can talk," Bates said. "You missed him that much?"

To Davis' surprise, Calvin lifted his chin. Not enough to look Bates in the eyes, but enough to show him that he wasn't cowering. "I did. I was worried about him. He left without telling me where he was going, just that he'd eventually be back. I couldn't allow that to happen."

Bates barked out a laugh. "Allow that to happen? Who's the one in charge in your relationship?"

God, Davis hated this. Still, he straightened and gently

pushed Calvin behind him. "I am, of course. But I get why he worried. I should have told him what was happening. The mistake was mine."

Bates tapped his fingertips on the desk, and Davis took a second look at the other man. Devon had described his ex-boyfriend, Elroy, and Davis was pretty sure that was who was sitting with Bates. He couldn't be a hundred percent sure, but what were the odds? This guy wasn't a Beast, or at least, not one who lived in the house. He could be living in another house that belonged to the gang, but he looked like the description Devon had given of Elroy.

There was nothing Davis could do about it, though. He would tell Bran about Elroy's presence here, but so far, he couldn't give Bran any details about what Elroy and Bates were planning for Gillham, unfortunately. After what had happened today, he didn't think he would ever become a gang member. Even if Bates didn't kick him out right away, as a prospect, this was a mess he'd made, and he couldn't come back from it.

"Are you sending him home?" Bates asked.

Davis shrugged as if it didn't matter to him whether or not Calvin left. "I can."

"But you'd rather have him here."

Davis stroked his hand down Calvin's back and squeezed his ass, grinning at Bates. "Well, there's a reason I bonded with him, and it's not only because we're mates."

Bates laughed again, and the sound made Davis' skin crawl. "True that. I was told you didn't partake of the ladies who come around, and it makes sense now."

"I might have if they'd been boys, but this is easier. He already knows what I like. I don't have to train him."

Davis hoped Calvin understood what he was doing. He had to play along, even though he hated the words he was saying. He would never be with another man for the rest of his life, and that would have happened even if he and Calvin hadn't been bonded. They were mates, and Davis respected that bond. He never wanted to hurt Calvin, even though he knew he would, eventually. But not like this. He would never cheat on Calvin, not even for a job.

Bates raked a hand through his longish hair. "Yes, well. You're allowed to have him here if that's what you want, but keep him on a leash. I don't want any more problems. Got it?"

Davis' heart raced as he nodded. "Got it. I'll make sure he understands what's going on here. He won't step out of line again."

"Make sure that doesn't happen. Now leave. I have a meeting."

Davis wished he were a fly on the wall so he could listen in, but instead, he grabbed Calvin's hand and pulled him out of the office. They both needed to get out of the house, at least for a bit. They'd been ordered to stay away for today, and that was more than okay with Davis. If he could choose, he'd never come back here. He couldn't, choose that, though.

Or maybe he could.

He waited until he and Calvin were back to his apartment to look at Calvin. "That went okay," he said.

Calvin snorted. "I thought he was going to kill us."

"It was a possibility. I'm not going to lie to you."

"Well, we were lucky he didn't do it. What now? Do I have to play the submissive little boy for you?"

Davis bit his lower lip. "I need to call Bran. I have to tell him what happened."

Calvin grimaced. "I bet that's going to go down well with him. I'm sorry I messed things up."

Davis couldn't resist. He wrapped an arm around Calvin's shoulders and pulled him close, kissing his temple. "You did nothing wrong."

"I made a mess. That was wrong."

"But we're okay. Both of us. And I still have the job."

"You want to continue? I wish we could go back home."

Davis would go if Calvin asked. Calvin was more important than any job. "*You* certainly could. I'll tell Bates I ordered you to go home. I'll say I didn't want you to be a distraction, or whatever. But *I* have to stay."

Calvin sighed. "I thought you'd say that. Call Bran. The sooner you're done with this, the better it will be."

He was right, so Davis called Bran right away and explained to him what had happened. Bran wasn't happy, but he agreed that they did things the best way possible, considering what Calvin had done. "Maybe you should come home, both of you," he said.

Davis looked at Calvin, who was listening to the conversation. "Both of us? Not just Calvin?"

"I don't know if I want to risk it. They might have fallen for your story, but it's still going to create problems. I'm ready to bet that at least a few members, if not Bates himself, will keep an extra eye on you. Do you really want to have to work with that?"

"So you want both of us to come home?"

"I would feel more comfortable, sure. But it's your decision."

Davis opened his mouth to ask Calvin, but to his surprise, Calvin shook his head. "I want to fix this," he said.

Davis put a hand on the phone so Bran wouldn't have to listen to the conversation. "You did nothing wrong. Nothing is messed up. You don't have to be here. This isn't your job. It's mine."

Calvin crossed his arms over his chest and glared at Davis. "That doesn't mean I can't help."

"I don't want you to get hurt."

"And *I* don't want *you* to get hurt. We're not going

anywhere. Gillham is my home. It's *our* home. I won't allow anyone to destroy it, not even the Beasts."

Davis dropped his hand from the phone. "Calvin wants to stay."

"I hope you know what you're doing."

Davis hoped they did, too. He wasn't sure what he'd do if something happened to Calvin, but it wouldn't be pretty, that was for sure.

Calvin hoped he wasn't making the biggest mistake of his life by wanting to stay. He wasn't sure what would happen, but he needed Davis to finish this. He wouldn't be able to live with himself if Davis had to leave the job because of him and something happened to the pack, the town, or anyone Calvin knew.

He'd only arrived in Gillham recently, and he was still settling down, but the town had become a safe haven for him, and he didn't want to lose it. It was a place in which Nate felt comfortable, the place in which he had a business, and Calvin didn't want him to lose that. He didn't want *anyone* to lose the town. It had its problems, just like every town in the country, but it was a nice place to live, especially as a shifter. Calvin knew that everyone in Gillham would accept him, and those who didn't would keep their mouth shut because they wouldn't want anyone to think they were bigots.

That was why he was staying. That was why he wanted Davis to finish this. He still wasn't sure it was a good idea, and he was terrified, but he wanted to do this.

"We should go to bed," Davis said. He was sitting on the other side of the couch as he and Calvin watched TV, and things were awkward between them, to say the least. They hadn't touched since the phone call with Bran, and Calvin didn't know what had happened. Nate was no doubt pissed that Calvin was gone, but Calvin knew he hadn't been given details. It was vital for Davis' undercover mission to stay as secret as possible, and unfortunately, that meant Nate didn't know where Calvin was or when he would come back.

Was Davis angry with Calvin for wanting to stay? Or maybe for barging in the way he had? He knew he shouldn't have, but he wasn't regretting it, not yet anyway. Maybe the awkwardness between him and Davis was only because they were new mates. They might have bonded, and Calvin didn't regret it, but they were still trying to find their way around each other. Calvin was uncomfortable with a lot, and he knew Davis wanted to shield him, to protect him against the world, and against himself if that was what Calvin needed.

The problem was that Calvin wasn't sure what he needed.

He wanted a real relationship with Davis. They were mates, and they were bonded. Surely they should sit close while they watched TV at the very least? Calvin couldn't remember the last time he'd had a relationship, but he was pretty sure that was how things went.

He understood why Davis wasn't pushing for more, but he wasn't sure how to get him to get over it. He wanted to tell Davis that he was okay, that he could take more than a kiss on the temple and a stroke on his back, but would Davis even believe him? Or would he think that Calvin was saying it just because he thought he had to?

Calvin didn't have an answer to that, and he wouldn't get one until he talked to Davis.

Davis rose from the couch and stretched, and Calvin couldn't help his wandering gaze. It had been a long time since he'd looked at a man that way. It had been a long time since he'd wanted anything sexual. He'd thought he'd lost that when he'd been in the labs, but he wasn't surprised that his mate was the one who could wake up his dead libido.

And waking it up he had. Calvin's cock was thickening in

his jeans at the sight of Davis stretching. It was true that Davis had exposed a stripe of skin on his back, but that hadn't been enough to get Calvin hard since he was a teenager. Davis made him see the world as if it was new, and while Calvin was confused, awkward, and unsure, he wouldn't change that for anything in the world. He wanted Davis. He wanted his mate, in his life and in his bed, and possibly, in his ass, too.

Davis turned to look at Calvin. "You can take the bedroom. I'll be okay on the couch."

Calvin looked down. There was no way Davis would be comfortable on the couch. It wasn't even big enough for him to stretch out. "Your feet will dangle off the side," Calvin pointed out.

"It doesn't matter. It won't be the first time I've slept in a weird position."

"But why? You don't have to."

"I don't want to make you uncomfortable."

"And you think I would be uncomfortable if we share the bed?"

Davis cocked his head. "Wouldn't you be?"

Calvin took his time to think about it. It had been so long since he'd shared a bed with anyone — more than ten years. He didn't count the cages he'd sometimes had to share with other people as sharing a bed, and he never would. Besides, he hadn't wanted to do that.

But he wanted to share the bed with Davis. God, he felt like an overgrown teenager with his dick getting hard every time the wind shifted, but that was how he felt, and he had to let Davis know. "I can't promise you I won't freak out. You know what happened to me, and how long it's been since I've had anyone in my life. But we're mates. I want us to share the bed if you're okay with it."

Davis blinked. "Okay with it? Of course I am. I've never wanted anything more than to have you in my bed. But I thought it would be more comfortable if I stayed away from you."

"I don't know what I'll be comfortable with. It's been a while since I've been comfortable with anything, to be honest. But I don't want my past to change my future. I don't want it to influence my present."

Davis offered Calvin a hand, and Calvin took it. He let his mate haul him off the couch, and he leaned close to Davis, needing his strength. "We don't have to do anything," Davis murmured. "The only thing I want is for you to be happy. I don't care what that entails. I'm ready to do it."

Calvin chuckled. "I would be careful if I were you. What if I have a kink you're not into?"

Davis' chest moved with his laughter. "A kink? Like what?"

Calvin grinned up at Davis. This was easy. He hadn't thought it would be, but it was. "Well, considering me, and considering you, I might be into daddy kink."

Davis' eyes widened. "Do you need me to be your daddy?"

Calvin burst out laughing. "No, I don't. But you're definitely a bear. I like it."

"I don't care what I am, as long as you're comfortable with me."

"I can't promise you I will be, but I want to try. I know you'll keep me safe, and that we won't do anything that makes me uncomfortable, or more uncomfortable than I already am. I want to do this. Please." It probably wasn't the best moment considering everything that was happening, but Calvin was convinced. He wanted this. He needed to show himself and Davis that he could do it.

Davis was still holding Calvin's hand, and he pulled him along the short hallway toward his bedroom. Calvin hated the apartment, and he wished they were somewhere else, although where, he didn't know.

Certainly not in his small bedroom in Nate's apartment. That would make things even more awkward. And maybe not in Davis' room in the enforcers building. There were too many people around, and Calvin wasn't sure he'd be able to do anything in that situation. But anywhere but here would have been better. Still, he didn't have a choice, so he decided to go along with it.

They settled into bed after taking their turns in the bathroom, and it was definitely more awkward than it had been before. They were both in their underwear, since Calvin hadn't thought to pack anything to bring with him when he'd left Gillham, and every time Davis moved, Calvin imagined he could feel their skin brushing together. It made him hard, and he needed more. He wasn't sure how to ask, though. He didn't know if he could, or if Davis would give him what he needed.

"They never touched me, not in the way you might think," Calvin blurted out. He wasn't sure why he was talking about it, but it felt like the right thing to do.

There was a pause before Davis asked, "In the lab, you mean?"

"Yeah. I know people who were sexually abused while they were there. A lot of the scientists were there because of science, but not all of them. And there were also the guards and the lab technicians. None of those people were good people, and some took advantage of their power. I was one of the lucky ones." It sounded odd, because he'd definitely been through hell, but he couldn't deny it.

"Even though they didn't touch you in a sexual way, it doesn't mean they didn't traumatize you."

Calvin started. "Oh, I'm traumatized, all right. What I was trying to say was that you don't have to hesitate to touch me if you want to. You can kiss me. Sex isn't a problem for me."

Davis rolled to his side, and even though it was dark,

Calvin knew he was looking at him. "What are you trying to say?"

"I don't know." Calvin really didn't. "But I know you won't hurt me. It's not just because you're my mate, but because you're a good man. I want more. I want to finally start my life. I've been waiting for something, and I don't know what. But I'm free now. I'm not in the labs, and I want more than the half-life I've been living. I want to take charge, and this feels like a good way to do that."

And that meant that Calvin had to take the first step. He had no idea what he was doing, but he pushed the blanket away and twisted to straddle Davis' waist. At the same time, Davis moved toward Calvin, and they hit their foreheads together. Pain exploded in Calvin's head, and he jerked back. "Oww."

"Shit. Are you okay?" Davis gently pulled Calvin's hand away from his face, and Calvin blinked at him. It was still dark, of course, so he couldn't see anything. He knew that Davis was worried, though. "I've been better. Your head feels like it's made of cement. Maybe marble?"

Davis huffed a laugh. "It's made of bone, just like yours. But seriously. Are you okay?"

Calvin couldn't help but chuckle. "I guess I'm more of a mess than I thought. I told you it had been a while since I'd done this."

"Then we can wait for as long as you need to."

But Calvin didn't want to. He didn't want to waste more time. He never wanted to wait when it came to Davis, and his fear would make that happen. He couldn't let the fear rule him, though, not anymore. He wanted more, and he would get it.

He leaned down to kiss Davis again, and this time, they managed not to bump into each other. Their lips met, and Calvin smiled. This was what he wanted. This was what he *needed.*

Davis didn't move, clearly letting Calvin set the pace.

Calvin wasn't sure how fast to go. He wanted everything, and he wanted it now, but he knew he wasn't ready for it. It would take him some time to get used to having people this close again, and that included Davis, even though he was Calvin's mate and they were bonded.

Bonded. It was hard to believe. A few weeks ago, Calvin wouldn't have thought this possible, yet here he was, kissing his mate and about to do more. How much more, he wasn't sure, but more.

Davis' hands were firm on Calvin's hips but not pushy. Calvin knew Davis would take anything Calvin was ready for and wouldn't demand anything more, and that was empowering. Calvin was the one in charge, something that hadn't happened in far too long.

He reached between them, shuddering at the feeling of Davis' hard cock pressing against the soft cotton of his boxer-briefs. He hadn't been sure sharing the bed wearing only underwear was a good idea, but now he was grateful for it. It only took him a few seconds to fish Davis' cock out, then his. He hissed at the touch of sensitive skin against sensitive skin and pressed closer to Davis while never letting go of his lips. He needed more friction, and he was grateful when Davis finally moved to wrap his big hand around both their cocks.

It was a little hard to think after that. Calvin had a hard time focusing on anything that wasn't what Davis' hand was doing to him. Davis' hold was firm and strong, just tight enough to drive Calvin crazy.

And crazy he went. He thrust into Davis' hand, forgetting about everything else. Having Davis so close to him, skin against skin, was maddening and almost too much. Calvin chased his release, the pleasure, without thinking about anything that wasn't his dick. And when he came, he pressed himself against Davis, burying his face against Davis' neck and bit down. They were already bonded, but Davis shuddered under Calvin and came, too, adding his seed to the puddle already slicking their stomachs.

Calvin flopped on top of Davis. He had no energy left to roll off, and since Davis was still breathing, it was probably fine.

Probably.

"Am I too heavy?" Calvin grumbled.

Davis laughed, his chest jerking Calvin up and down. "Nope. You're as light as a feather. We'll get stuck together if we don't clean up, though."

Calvin lightly slapped Davis' chest. "I'll get up eventually. But do you know how long it's been since I've done this? More than ten years. I'm going to need a moment."

Davis stroked his fingertips up and down Calvin's back, and Calvin's cock made a valiant effort at hardening again. "Take your time. I'm not going anywhere."

And that was enough for Calvin to finally breathe out and relax.

CHAPTER FIVE

Davis wanted to go home. He would even make do with going back to the apartment, where Calvin was waiting for him.

Calvin had been hiding there since he'd arrived. Thankfully, Bates hadn't demanded to see him again, and Davis hoped that would continue. He didn't want those two sides of his life to meet. He didn't want Calvin to be in even more danger than he was.

It was already bad enough. They couldn't go home, because Calvin wanted Davis to finish this job, and that meant Calvin was in danger twenty-four seven, no matter how hard Davis tried to protect him. And he was working hard on that. He was also working on becoming part of the Beasts, and that part, he hated, even more now that Calvin was with him. He hated having to move drugs around the city. He hated waiting all the time, expecting the Beasts to tell him to kill someone or do something just as bad. He could feel the Beasts' stain expanding to him, and he wanted it to stop. He still didn't have any answers for Bran, and that was a problem. He wasn't sure if Calvin's arrival had changed something, had made Davis seem less trustworthy, but it didn't matter. The situation was what it was, and Davis couldn't change it.

He wished he could, though.

He hated what he was doing to Calvin, and he'd tried to send Calvin back home several times. His mate was stubborn, though, and he wasn't budging. He would stay here until Davis was ready to leave, too, and nothing Davis could do or say would change that. It made Davis smile when he thought about it, even though it was frustrating. Calvin was as infuriating as he was gorgeous and lovable, and Davis couldn't wait for both of them to go back to Gillham and start a life together.

The situation was hard on Calvin. He hadn't said anything to Davis, but Davis would have had to be blind not to understand it. Calvin woke up every night with nightmares, and no matter how much Davis tried to help him, there was nothing he could do to stop those. He wanted to fight the memories. He wanted to help.

But he couldn't.

So instead, he made sure Calvin ate and slept enough. He was there for him when he had nightmares. He soothed him during the night. He made sure Calvin knew he was safe with him and tried to calm him down when he got anxious and overly worried. The situation didn't help, though, and Davis knew that eventually, something would break.

He hoped it wouldn't be Calvin. No matter how hard his mate was trying to show how strong he was, that wouldn't last forever. Davis needed to take Calvin away, but he knew better than to suggest it again. Calvin would say no, and Davis didn't want him to think that he believed him to be powerless or weak.

That couldn't be further from the truth.

Davis was trying to help Calvin learn how to shift, and even though the results weren't the same from one day to another, Calvin was taking huge steps forward. He didn't see it that way, of course, but Davis did. Calvin had become a shifter when he'd already been an adult. He'd never been taught to shift or to fly. It wasn't a bad thing. It wasn't his fault, and he was trying hard to change things. They were both working and making do with the situation, and it had to be enough.

"Prospect."

Davis froze on his way out of the gang house. "Yes?" He didn't want to talk to Bates, but he couldn't leave, not when Bates was stopping him. Bates would have his ass if he did, and not in a fun way.

Davis turned to face the leader of the Beasts. Bates looked him up and down, then asked, "How's your boy?"

Davis blinked. That wasn't what he'd expected, and he wasn't sure what to do about it, or how to feel. Bates was the enemy, and the fact that he was friendly didn't mean anything. "He's doing okay."

Bates nodded. "Good. There's a party tonight."

"I'm aware of that." And Davis hadn't been planning on attending, even though he knew it would be frowned upon.

"Bring him."

Shit. "I'm sure he already has plans."

"Does he? Do I have to ask again who's in charge in your relationship?"

Of course Bates thought Davis dominated Calvin, that he and Calvin weren't equal. He thought Davis was the boss, and Davis hadn't said anything to make him change his mind. Maybe that would keep Calvin safe.

But it also led to this kind of problem. "I'll tell him to come," Davis said. There was no way out of it. He could come up with a fake illness, but he doubted Bates would take his word for it. *No.* Calvin had to come, and Davis wasn't sure how to deal with that.

"Good. We'll be expecting you in a few hours. Go get your boy."

Bates turned away and left, and Davis released a breath.

That was the last thing he and Calvin needed. There wasn't a way out of it, though, so Davis headed home, wondering how he would tell Calvin about it. He knew Calvin would do everything he could to help, but Davis hated that he'd put him in this situation. He wanted to protect him, not to put him in the hands of the Beasts. The Beasts were the worst people he could imagine Calvin spending any length of time with, and instead of going there, he wondered what would happen if he grabbed Calvin and went home.

Bates didn't know who he was. He wouldn't know where to look for them. He would be pissed, but Davis was only a prospect. He didn't doubt that eventually, Bates and the Beasts would forget about him, and he and Calvin could be happy together in Gillham.

But Calvin wouldn't agree to that. He wanted to see this through, and Davis didn't fully understand why.

"Cal?" Davis called out as soon as he was in the apartment.

Calvin's head popped up from the couch where he was stretched out. "Hey. How was your day?"

Davis snorted softly. "You make it sound like I went to the office."

"Well, this is your job. So? How did it go? You have anything for Bran?"

Davis sighed and leaned against the back of the couch. "I don't. They don't trust me yet." He hesitated. He could avoid telling Calvin about the demand, and Calvin would never find out that Bates wanted him at the house. But Davis suspected that Bates would eventually come to look for them. The man didn't like to be disobeyed, and he'd been clear. He wanted Calvin and Davis to be at the party, and if they weren't there, he would notice it. He always did. "There's a party tonight at the house," Davis said.

Calvin sat up straighter and blinked. "Yes?"

"I thought I would be able to get out of it, but Bates stopped me before I could leave." Davis swallowed. He hated being the one to put his mate in danger. "He wants both of us there."

Calvin frowned. "Me too?"

"Yeah. You made an impression when you arrived, and he

was very specific. He wants me to drag you to the party, willing or not."

Calvin rubbed his face. "I don't want to go."

"And you don't have to. I can make an excuse. I could tell Bates that you're sick or something like that."

"And it'll work?"

Davis' shoulders slumped. "It won't. He'll demand to see you either way. I'm sorry, Calvin. Maybe you should have gone home to the pack."

Calvin rose from the couch and walked around it. He wrapped his arms around Davis' waist and leaned closer, pressing his cheek to Davis' chest. "I couldn't leave you alone here, not in this situation. I don't regret it, Davis. I don't think I ever will. And while it's true I'm not looking forward to this party or to spending any length of time with the Beasts, I'll do it. I know it's important for you and for the job, and I don't want you to get hurt if Bates decides to come looking for me."

"I wish you didn't have to do this," Davis murmured as he stroked a hand up and down Calvin's back.

"I wish you didn't have to do it, either. But I'll be careful, and I'll stick with you. I promise. I know how dangerous they are. I'll stick with you, and we'll be out of there as soon as possible."

Davis nodded. He wanted nothing more than to send Calvin back home. He wouldn't force his mate to leave, though. Calvin had already been through enough with people forcing him to do things, and the last thing he needed was for his mate to do the same.

But Davis was worried. He hoped everything would be okay, but he couldn't promise that to his mate, and that made him anxious. They were going to go to the party. They had to.

But if Davis had anything to say about it, tonight would be the last night they spent with the Beasts. He'd had enough. He wanted to take Calvin home, and nothing would stop him from doing just that.

When Calvin thought about parties, this wasn't what he had in mind. At first sight, it looked like your run-of-the-mill party. There was music, people milling around and talking, laughing, and a few even dancing. But when he looked closer, he could see that it wasn't just a party.

Calvin looked away from the men doing drugs and pressed closer to Davis. He didn't want to be here. He wanted to go home, and by home, he didn't mean the apartment he and Davis were sharing right now.

Davis wrapped an arm around Calvin's shoulders and pulled him close. "You okay?" he asked. He had to shout over the music for Calvin to hear him.

Calvin nodded. He didn't want to speak. He wasn't sure he could speak, not with the knot in his throat. He felt like he was about to throw up, and he knew he couldn't. He couldn't embarrass Davis that way, not when the Beasts were eyeing him like he was a puzzle to solve—or break.

He still didn't understand why Bates wanted him there at the party. It didn't make sense. He'd met the man once, and only for a few minutes. Bates had taken an interest in him, but not beyond wondering why he was here.

And now Calvin was at the party because Bates had wanted him to be. What did it mean?

Davis leaned down, kissed Calvin's forehead, then asked, "Cal? Please tell me you're okay." He paused. "Just say you're not, and I'm taking you away. I promise. We don't have to stay if you're uncomfortable."

Calvin shook his head. "We have to. Bates wants us here, and you know what that means."

"I'm not going to allow him or anyone else to hurt you. I promise."

Calvin nodded. He wouldn't be here if he was on his own, but he trusted Davis. Davis would protect him, and that was the most important thing.

Calvin was grateful when Davis dragged him toward the wall. He grabbed two beers, still sealed, and handed one to Calvin after opening it. Together, they leaned against the wall and watched the people around them.

Calvin was pretty sure they were the only same-sex couple, and that was okay. He didn't care how accepting the Beasts were. As far as he was concerned, they needed to pay for what they'd done, and being accepting of gay people wouldn't change that. Besides, he doubted they *actually* accepted Davis. They hadn't said anything because they'd been ordered to keep their mouths shut, and because from what Calvin knew, Bates swung both ways. But Calvin didn't fool himself into thinking that they wouldn't stab Davis in the back if they had the chance to do it, which was why he stuck with Davis the entire evening.

It wasn't like Calvin wanted to party anyway. He didn't like parties. There were too many people, too many noises. The yells and laughter brought him back to the time he'd spent in the labs, and he wanted to go home and forget about all of this. He couldn't, though, and he'd been the one to put himself in the situation. He'd been the one to insist that he could do this, and now, he would show Davis that he could.

"Look there," Davis murmured as he moved even closer.

Calvin suspected that anyone looking at them would think they were kissing, but they weren't. Davis' mouth was close to Calvin's ear so that Calvin could hear what he was saying, and it took him a few seconds to understand what Davis was talking about.

"You mean Bates?" he asked.

"That guy he's with? It's Elroy."

Calvin frowned. "Devon's ex?"

"Yeah, him. Or at least, I think so. He fits the description Devon gave us, and he's working with the Beasts."

Calvin watched as Elroy and Bates disappeared down the hallway that led to Bates's office. "You think they're having a meeting?"

"It sure looks like it."

Calvin gently pushed Davis away. "We should spy on them."

"How are we supposed to do that?"

Calvin looked around. He knew how they could do it, but he wasn't sure he could pull it off. "Do you trust me?"

Davis frowned. "Of course I trust you. More than anyone else in the world."

That made Calvin's heart race, but he forced himself to ignore that and any emotion Davis created in him. "Good." He took Davis' hand and dragged him toward the hallway.

He'd only been here once, but Davis had told him about the house, and Calvin knew where every door they passed led, and what every single room was. Davis had wanted to be sure he could find a way out if anything happened, and Calvin was grateful for the knowledge now. That meant that he knew there was a backroom between the living room and Bates's office. It was a mix between a pantry and the backroom of the bar at Nate's, and it was oddly familiar to Calvin.

"Where are we going?" Davis asked, looking around slightly frantically.

"The backroom,"

Calvin slammed the door shut behind them and leaned against it. He took a second to breathe. "You think anyone noticed us?"

Davis frowned. "I don't know. Maybe. What are we doing here, Calvin?"

Calvin pointed at the AC duct on the wall. "This. I'm going

to shift, and I'm going to go to Bates' office. You'll stay here and make enough noise that people will think we're having sex."

Davis' eyes widened. "You can't do that."

"Why not?"

"Because it's dangerous."

"Everything is dangerous right now. Being here. Being with the Beasts. Even breathing. This is a way to leave and go back home. If we can find out what Bates and Elroy are planning, we can go back. We can tell the pack to be careful and what to look for. Whatever you're doing isn't working."

"It might not be working, but it's my job. I'm doing what I was ordered to do."

"Maybe. That doesn't mean it's the right thing to do, though. We have to improvise. Playing prospect and praying that they won't ask you to do anything you're not willing to do isn't going to work for much longer. Something needs to change, and that's why I'm here." It wasn't what Calvin had been planning when he'd decided to come, but he wanted to help. He could do it.

Or at least, he hoped he could.

He had to ignore the feelings of being powerless and weak, the feelings that he wouldn't be able to do this. He had to ignore the tiny voice in the back of his head telling him that he was going to get himself killed, or worse, that Davis would get hurt because of what Calvin was doing.

Calvin knew this was the only thing they could do right now. If they ignored this chance and they went back to the party and acted as if nothing was going on, who knew how long this job would last. Calvin wanted to take Davis away from here, and this was his chance to make that happen.

He just needed to get over what he felt. He knew he wasn't powerless. He might not be the greatest at shifting, and he might suck at flying, but he could do this. He was sure of it.

He quickly stripped, and Davis' eyes went even wider, something Calvin hadn't thought was possible. "Calvin, you can't do this."

Nothing he was saying would convince Calvin otherwise, though.

Calvin thrust his clothes into Davis' arms. "Okay. I *can* do this. I know you're worried, and so am I, but I promise I won't put myself in danger. Okay?"

"Just being here puts you in danger."

"I know that. Let me focus, okay?" Calvin closed his eyes before Davis could say anything. He expected Davis to continue to protest, but instead, Davis stayed quiet. His presence next to Calvin was soothing, and even though Calvin was still worried and anxious, it was easier than usual to focus on the shift.

Calvin had been trying to learn to shift ever since he'd arrived in Gillham. Hell, he'd been trying to do it for years. Controlling his shift would have meant he could be free from the lab sooner, but so far, it had been hard to do with no one to tell him what to do or what to look out for. But Davis had been working with him, and Calvin knew he could do it.

He knew the exact moment he became a bat. His body shrank, and he felt odd—his body not the same as he was used to.

He opened his eyes, and Davis towered over him.

Calvin was a small bat, but he *was* a bat, and that meant he could fly, or at the very least, he could *try* to fly.

He focused on his wings and batted them. It took him a second to get the gist of it, but once he did, it was fairly easy to rise in the air.

Davis dropped Calvin's clothes and sprang into action, opening the duct, putting the grate on the floor, and gently taking Calvin in his hands, holding him up to the duct. "Be careful. Please." Davis stroked a finger down Calvin's furry back, and Calvin shuddered.

He needed this to be over so he could take Davis home.

He didn't look back as he flew through the duct. He couldn't, because he didn't want to change his mind. Luckily for him, he didn't have to fly for long. The backroom was close to Bates' office, and it didn't take more than a few minutes for Calvin to get to another AC exit.

From where he was, he could see into the office. Bates was behind his desk, with Elroy on the other side of it. They were talking, and they looked entirely comfortable. Calvin didn't think they knew he was spying on them, and he hoped they wouldn't find out. He wasn't sure he would make it out of this alive if they did.

"When will everything be ready?" Elroy asked.

"A few more weeks."

"Weeks? This has already taken too much time."

Bates arched a brow. "Are you trying to tell me how to do my job?"

"No." Elroy sounded disgruntled. "But you promised you could take out the pack and the rest of the town. I want you to do that."

"And I will. But as I'm sure you're aware, it's going to take more than the people I have here to make that happen. This needs to be planned to the second if we don't want things to be fucked up. You want to destroy the pack? Good. But you're going to have to follow my lead."

Elroy grunted. "Fine. Tell me." Calvin held his breath and listened.

Davis hated this. Usually, he was the one in the middle of things. He was the one who did what Calvin was doing right now. He hated feeling like he didn't have control, but even more, he hated the thought that he might lose Calvin.

What could happen to him? What would Bates do if he found him? Davis already knew the answer to that, and he didn't want to think about it. He didn't want it to happen.

He took a deep breath and forced himself to focus on the AC duct. He needed to be ready to grab Calvin as soon as he dropped out of it. They needed to get out of here, and they needed to do it fast. Even if Bates and Elroy didn't notice Calvin listening to them, they couldn't linger here.

Davis remembered that Calvin told him to act as if they were having sex, so he banged on the door a few times and moaned. He felt ridiculous, but it had to be done. "Come on, baby. Suck my dick," he said, keeping his voice rough.

He rolled his eyes at the laughter that came from behind the door, then banged against it a few more times.

Once that was done, he went back to the open duct. This was taking too long. *Jesus*. Davis needed to do something. What, though? He couldn't go into the duct himself. He couldn't call for Calvin because he'd risk him being found. He was powerless, just like Calvin had felt before.

He reached for his phone, wondering if Bran could help, but before he could take it out of his pocket, someone behind him said, "We should go."

Davis jumped, his heart racing, and he twirled around to look at Calvin. "When did you leave the duct?"

"Just now. Come on. Give me my clothes. We need to get out of here."

Davis obeyed. "Did you find anything?"

"I have a list of names and the plan. I don't know if I'll remember all of them, but I'll try. I don't feel comfortable hanging around, though."

"We won't. Now that you know what's going to happen, we can go home. We'll go to the apartment, and as soon as we're there, we'll call Bran. He'll send someone to pick us up, and the Beasts won't even know we're gone until tomorrow."

Calvin's head popped through his t-shirt. "What's going to happen when they realize you're gone? Aren't they going to suspect you found out what they're planning?"

"Possibly, but it's a risk we need to take."

Calvin nodded and pulled up his jeans, then shoved his feet into his shoes. Davis grabbed Calvin and pulled him close, messing his hair and kissing him hard. Calvin gasped, but he didn't push Davis away. Davis tried to be as fast as he could. He needed to make it look as if Calvin had been kissed and as he if he'd blown Davis.

"What was that for?" Calvin asked when Davis took a step back.

"We were having sex in here, remember?" He hesitated. "A blowjob. At least, that's what I made it sound like."

"Great." Calvin licked his lips until they were shining with saliva. "How do I look? Debauched?"

Davis wanted to drag Calvin to bed, but right now, they had other things to focus on. He pulled Calvin close again and kissed him, then released him and took his hand. "Yeah. Ready to go?"

Calvin nodded. Davis could feel how tense he was by the hold he had on his hand, and he hoped being away from the house would help him relax. He took a deep breath and opened the door, then pulled Calvin along.

Only a few people noticed them passing through the living room. Davis got a few winks and snickers, but no one tried to stop them, not after he announced that he needed to fuck Calvin and that he was taking him home to do just that for the rest of the night. Bates was still in the office and wouldn't come out until he was done with Elroy. That gave Davis and Calvin a little time to go home and to get out of town.

"That was easier than I expected," Calvin murmured when they reached the bike.

"We're still not out of danger."

95

"I know. But leaving the house and the Beasts behind feels good."

Davis couldn't deny that. This was it. This was the day he'd go home, and he was going home with his mate. There was nothing he wanted more.

He was careful as he drove them home, but he pushed the speed limit. He couldn't risk Bates understanding what had happened before they were out of the apartment. Davis hadn't told anyone where he lived, but he didn't doubt that at least a few Beasts had been ordered to follow him home after that first day. They knew where to find him if they needed him, and they *would* need him if they realized that someone had been spying on them. Hopefully, someone would give Bates the excuse that Davis had dragged his mate home to fuck him, but Davis couldn't count on that. He didn't want to in case it wasn't enough.

"What did you learn?" he asked as soon as he and Calvin were in front of the apartment building. He hadn't even dismounted the bike yet.

"They're going to attack Gillham and destroy the pack," Calvin rubbed his face. "They don't have enough people yet, which is why they haven't acted on it. But they're getting there."

That was definitely enough to go home. "You said you have names?"

"I do. There's Elroy, of course, and I have others. I don't know how useful it's going to be, and I don't have a date, but hopefully, this is enough."

"Knowing the pack and the town will be attacked is a lot, yes. Gillham will need us there, not here."

"Let's go home, then," Calvin said as he took Davis' hand.

They walked up the stairs together, both of them nervous. Davis checked every single corner and every shadow they passed, just in case, and Calvin was way too jumpy, but they made it to the apartment.

Davis hated leaving the bike behind, but it wasn't even his. Besides, Bran would no doubt send a Nix to grab it.

"Put everything in the backpacks," he told Calvin as soon as they were inside the apartment. "I'm going to call Bran. Be ready to leave in five minutes."

Calvin nodded and disappeared into the bedroom while Davis took his phone out. He dialed Bran's number from memory, then bounced his foot as he waited for him to answer.

"Davis? Is everything okay?" Bran asked, his voice careful yet tense, even at this hour of the night.

"We have something. We need to get out of here."

"I'll send someone right away. Be ready."

"We will."

Davis wasn't sure how good what Calvin had found out was, but now that he knew why the Beasts and Elroy hadn't attacked yet, it might give them a chance. They had names, and that meant they could take out people before they could help Elroy and Bates. If the problem Bates had was numbers, that could be fixed by the enforcers.

They weren't professional killers, but Davis was more than happy to become one if it meant keeping Gillham and the pack safe.

This was it. He and Calvin were about to get out of here. They were going to go back to their lives. It wouldn't be a normal life since they would have to get ready for what was coming, but it was better than what they had here.

Davis couldn't wait. He wanted to leave all of this behind and be happy. That might not happen right away, but it would be soon enough, once Gillham was safe.

Calvin was so unsure of himself, yet he'd been the one to find all of this. He'd be the one to save Gillham if they managed to make that happen. He wasn't powerless. He was strong, and Davis needed him to believe that. He was going to tell Calvin that as many times as he needed to for Calvin to believe him, even if it took years.

Davis couldn't wait to spend those years right next to Calvin, being happy with him.

They needed to get out. Calvin couldn't wait. He wanted to go home and leave the Beasts far behind. He never wanted to think about them again if he could.

He knew it was ridiculous and that he would have to talk about what had happened again and again, but it didn't matter. As long as he was back in Gillham, he would be fine. He had to be.

"Do you have a lot of stuff left to pack?" Davis asked from the bedroom door.

Luckily, Calvin had arrived with nothing, and even though he'd been here a few weeks, he hadn't bought a lot. He had just enough clothes for a few days, and everything he owned in the apartment fit into one small backpack.

He raised it so Davis could see it. "I'm all done. We can go."

Davis nodded and headed to the living room, and Calvin followed him. Davis had already called Bran, and a Nix was waiting for him in the living room. Calvin thought he recognized her from the bar. She was probably part of Davis' team, from the way they greeted each other, but Calvin didn't have time to ask. He didn't want to spend one more second than necessary in the apartment and in the same town as the Beasts.

He only relaxed once they arrived back in Gillham. He wasn't surprised to see a man was waiting for them, but he still took a step back when the man moved toward them. He was relieved when Davis stepped in front of him, even though he knew he wasn't in danger.

"Davis? Are you and Calvin okay?" the man asked.

Calvin was slightly offended by the fact that the man wasn't talking to him directly, but he supposed he shouldn't be considering how he'd reacted just now.

Davis nodded. "We're fine. We had to get out of there, though."

"You said on the phone that you have news."

"We do." Davis wrapped an arm around Calvin's shoulders. "Or rather, he does. He did all the work."

Calvin looked at his feet, then forced himself to look up at the man, because he wasn't going to cower in front of anyone ever again after what he'd been through, "I didn't do all the work. I did what I could."

The man nodded and offered Calvin his hand, which Calvin shook. He knew he shouldn't be afraid. No one here would hurt him. "I'm Bran, the leader of the enforcers here in Gillham."

"Calvin."

Bran smiled. "I know you, Calvin. It's a pleasure to meet you."

"Same. Although I guess I wished things could be different."

To Calvin's surprise, Bran smiled instead of berating him for going after Davis without authorization.

"I have to say I'm not surprised you decided to follow Davis, especially now that I know you're mates." He looked at Davis. "I *was* surprised that you didn't tell me about it. You know I would have allowed you to stay."

Davis shrugged. "Sure, and who would you have sent instead of me? Everyone in my team is either mated or has a significant other, or something else that keeps them here. I was the only one free to go."

"Not entirely free."

"I only met Calvin after I agreed to do this, and I wasn't going to back down. Besides, this is a moot point by now. I went, did my thing, and came back with information." He paused and kissed Calvin's temple. "Or rather, *Calvin* came back with information. He seriously did all the work here."

That wasn't true, but Calvin was done protesting. If these two guys wanted to give him more credit than he was due, that was fine with him.

Bran gestured toward the door. "Why don't we head out? I'm sure the two of you can use some rest, and you can tell me what you learned on the way there."

Calvin agreed. He needed a bed in which he would feel safe. Sleeping with Davis had helped, but still, he hadn't felt safe since he'd left Gillham, and he hadn't yet had a good night's sleep because of that. He wanted to close his eyes and not open them for at least twelve hours, and that would only happen if he told Bran everything he now knew. "I spied on Bates and the guy he was with. Davis thinks it was Elroy."

Bran arched a brow, but that was the only sign he recognized Elroy's name. Calvin had no idea who the guy was beyond being Devon's ex, and he didn't care. If he was with Bates—with the Beasts—it meant he wasn't a good guy, and that was more than enough for Calvin. He didn't even need Devon to give him any details about why he was on the run. "I heard them talking. They're going to attack the town and the pack. They want to get rid of Kameron and everyone who lives here."

Bran nodded. "I'm not surprised. Do you have any details?"

"Not a lot. I have names, though. They're the people the Beasts are waiting for. They have a lot of members, but not enough to take on the entire pack and the enforcers who live here. So they've been putting together more fighters. I can give you all the names of the people who are supposed to bring their people along to the fight."

"Good. Maybe we can take those people out before the Beasts actually attack. We would probably be able to hold our own if they came, but the best would be to keep them away entirely."

Calvin didn't know a lot about strategy or fighting, but he understood what Bran was saying. The town and the pack were full of families, children, and elderly people who would get hurt if the Beasts came. The best bet to keep Gillham and the pack safe was to keep the Beasts away, by any means necessary. "Are you going to kill them?" he asked Bran.

He half expected Bran not to answer, but instead, Bran said, "It's possible. It will depend on who these people are. To be working with the Beasts, they can't be good people, but some of them might have been tricked into it or blackmailed. We're going to check all of them, of course, before making any kind of decisions. But you shouldn't worry about it. You did a job you weren't even hired for, and the pack and I owe you for that."

Calvin shrugged. "You sent my mate there. I wouldn't have gone otherwise."

Bran smiled. "Then maybe it's a good thing I sent him. Can you give me the list of names right now? That way, I won't have to disturb you anymore. I'm sure you want some sleep."

"If you have a piece of paper and a pen, sure."

Bran produced those two things from his pockets and handed them off to Calvin. Calvin hauled his backpack up his shoulder, but Davis was there, unhooking it and pulling it onto his own shoulder. He tilted his chin toward the notebook. "Write down everything you know. I can't wait to get into bed."

Calvin blushed, even though Davis probably hadn't meant his sentence the way Calvin had taken it. He focused on the notebook, writing down every single name he remembered and all the details.

It wasn't much. Elroy and Bates had been going over a list of associates and people who were on their side, which was how Calvin had gotten all those names. That was pretty much everything he'd gotten, though. Bates and Elroy hadn't mentioned any dates or strategy. Calvin wished he could do more, but he hoped that what he already had would help.

Calvin blinked when he stopped writing. He hadn't even looked at the enforcers' building as they walked through it. He wanted to go home to his bed, but he knew better than to do that now. Nate was probably pissed with him, and he would strangle him if Calvin popped up on his doorstep. He would be right, too. Calvin had left without telling anyone where he was going or why, and Nate had to be frantic. He probably had some words for Calvin, but Calvin hoped it could wait until the next morning.

He handed the list to Bran. "Here it is. It's everything I could remember. I'm sorry I don't have more."

Bran took the notebook and pen. "It's already more than we had before, so thank you. We wouldn't be here without you. Now go get some rest and food. Davis, no one should disturb you until tomorrow morning, so take your time. Welcome home, and thanks for what you did."

Calvin opened his mouth to thank Bran again, but Davis took his hand and dragged him into what must have been his bedroom, closing the door behind him. He dropped both backpacks, and Calvin looked around.

He hadn't expected much. He knew most of the enforcers lived here, so he'd thought Davis had a small room, maybe a communal bathroom. The room *was* small, but from an open door, he could see a private bathroom, and it made him smile. He didn't want to share a bathroom, or anything else. He'd had enough of that when he'd been in the labs.

"Have you changed your mind?" Davis asked.

Calvin blinked. Maybe it was because of how tired he was, but he didn't understand what Davis was talking about. "About what?"

"We bonded. We're together, right? I mean, as a couple."

Calvin didn't understand why Davis was bringing this up. "Of course we are. Why? Is there a problem?"

Davis shook his head. "I was just wondering if I needed to take you home to the bar."

Calvin took a step closer to Davis. "I'm not going anywhere unless you kick me out. Are you going to kick me out?"

"Of course not.

"Then I'm here to stay. We might have bonded because we needed to, but it doesn't mean I regret it. I don't. I want to be with you." Calvin wanted this after everything he'd lost. He *needed* it.

He knew he had a lot of work to do on himself, and that Davis wouldn't be able to help, but he wanted something of his own, something good in his life, something to work toward.

Any he did now. Davis, or rather, a healthy and loving relationship with him, was Calvin's goal. He would do everything he had to in order to reach that goal. He deserved it.

He deserved everything good that would happen to him, and no one would be able to convince him otherwise.

He lifted his arms and hooked them around Davis' shoulders. "Why don't we go to bed?"

Davis patted Calvin's back. "You should grab a shower."

"Are you saying I stink?"

Davis laughed, and Calvin laughed with him. Now that he wasn't constantly worrying about someone attacking him or finding out why Davis was there, it was easier to let go.

"No, just that I know you've been rushing through showers when we were at the apartment, and now you don't have to. I wish I had a tub, but I don't, so you'll have to make do with the shower. But you can take your time. I'll grab something to eat from downstairs in the meantime."

It sounded good, but not as much as what Calvin had in mind. He and Davis had been spending all their nights in the apartment in the same bed, but they'd never taken the time to explore each other's bodies. They hadn't been able to, not when someone could have barged in on them at any time.

Now they could, and Calvin wanted to take advantage of that.

Instead of letting go like Davis seemed to expect him to do, he dropped to his knees. There was a pit at the bottom of his stomach, but he ignored it, focusing on his mate instead. He didn't have a reason to be nervous. Even if he sucked at this — pun not intended — Davis wouldn't care.

"So you don't want to shower," Davis said, amusement tingeing his voice.

"We can do that and eat later." Calvin tilted his head to look Davis in the eyes as he opened his mate's jeans. "Unless you want me to stop?"

Davis slid his fingers into Calvin's hair. "Never."

That was good enough for Calvin. He pushed Davis' jeans and underwear down to the floor and found himself face to cock with Davis' dick. He licked his lips, wondering how it would taste, how it would feel on his tongue. There was only one way to find out.

Calvin leaned closer. He took a deep breath, inhaling his mate's scent, letting it soothe and calm him down as he opened his mouth. This wasn't his first blowjob, but it had been so long since he'd last given or received one that it might as well have been. It certainly felt like it.

He gave the cock in front of his nose a lick. Davis didn't move, and Calvin was grateful for that. He wasn't sure how he would have reacted if Davis had tried to pull him closer. Not well, that was for sure.

Calvin sucked in a breath and wrapped his lips around the head of Davis' cock. It felt odd, and his lips were stretched, but he remembered how to do this. He wrapped his fingers around the base and bobbed his head, making sure to use his tongue to alternatively stroke the head on his way up, then the length on his way down.

Davis moaned, and Calvin's chest filled with smugness. He was the one and only man who could do this from now on. He would be the only one Davis did this with. Davis was his, and it felt so damn good and reassuring. Davis was the one person Calvin never had to worry about. They were bonded mates, together forever, no matter what happened.

Calvin's jaw ached, and he had to stop. He sucked in a breath and moved toward Davis' cock again, but Davis stopped him with a gentle touch on the jaw. "Come up here." His voice was rough, and Calvin knew his would match, so he didn't try talking.

Instead, he rose to his feet and let Davis kiss him as if it were the first and last time. They were both breathless once Davis leaned back, and Calvin couldn't help but move closer. He wanted so much more.

"I want you inside me."

Calvin blinked, wondering if he'd spoken out loud. He was pretty sure he hadn't, though. "What?"

Davis smirked. "I want you inside me. I want to be filled by you."

Calvin *had* heard that right, then. "Are you sure?"

"I've never been surer of anything. We can do it the other way around if you want, or not at all. I want you to be comfortable with whatever we decide."

"I want to fuck you."

Davis laughed. "Got it. Uh, I have lube in the nightstand. No condoms, though. I don't do one-night stands, so I haven't done this in a while."

Calvin grinned. "We're shifters. We don't need condoms." At last, one good thing came from being a shifter.

Calvin went to the nightstand as Davis got rid of his clothes. Calvin had already seen his mate naked, but he didn't think he would ever tire of the sight. Davis was everything he'd ever dreamed of and more—tall, broad, hairy, and perfectly imperfect, Calvin's present and future. He looked even better naked and stretched out on the bed, and as soon as he was naked, too, Calvin crawled between his legs. He ran his hands up Davis' thighs, smiling at how the hair tickled his palms.

Then he got his mouth on Davis again. It felt good to be in charge, and Calvin was grateful Davis didn't try to stop him. Instead, he let him explore, and Calvin took joy in doing that. He mouthed the skin where Davis' thigh met his groin, he licked Davis' balls, and he tickled his hole with careful fingers until Davis was panting and pushing down for more.

"You're driving me crazy," Davis groaned. "You don't have to be so careful. You can fuck me."

Calvin kissed the inside of Davis' thigh. "I make the decisions. I don't want to rush into this. You deserve to be taken care of after you've taken care of me so much." And just as importantly, Calvin was finally in control.

He'd missed it, even though he hadn't realized it. He was retaking charge of his life, and it was thanks to Davis, at least in part. Calvin would always owe him that, and this was a tiny way to repay him—by making him lose his mind and giving him pleasure.

That lasted until Calvin finally pushed inside Davis. Davis was hot and tight, and everything Calvin could have dreamed of, spread under him with his cheeks flushed and his skin shining with sweat. He was smiling, and he opened his arms to Calvin, who dropped down as he pushed in.

Then they were one. It was a ridiculously sappy thought,

but they *were* linked, and they moved together, Davis undulating under Calvin, Calvin pushing in and out of him. Calvin had to force himself to hold back because he didn't want to come before Davis. He wanted to take care of his mate the way Davis has been taking care of him, so he did.

He moved slowly but firmly, driving Davis crazy. When Davis reached for his cock, Calvin let him, even though he wanted to be the one doing it. He didn't think he'd be able to coordinate everything, though, so he focused on moving in and out of Davis and on watching him as he jacked himself off until he came.

Davis pulsed around Calvin, and Calvin stopped resisting. He buried his face against Davis' neck and bit down. His teeth stayed human, and he didn't draw blood, but it was enough. He pushed one last time into Davis and came, their bodies twined together, still one.

Forever one.

Chapter Six

A loud bang made Davis jump off the bed. He was naked, but he didn't even care as he placed himself between the bed and the bedroom door, ready to protect Calvin if he needed to.

He blinked his eyes open, wondering what was happening, since the bedroom door was still closed. It took him a second to remember that they weren't in the apartment anymore, but rather, in the enforcers' building. That meant that whoever was knocking on the door didn't want to hurt them.

It sure sounded like they did, though.

"Open the door," someone bellowed.

Davis blinked, then reached for his jeans on the floor. He pulled them on, looked at Calvin, who was just waking up, then opened the door.

He was pushed aside by Nate, who stepped into the bedroom, looking around.

Davis didn't like being pushed around. "What do you want?" he snapped.

Nate faced him. "What I want? What do you think I want? My brother disappeared. No one knew where he was or what had happened. Then I hear that he's back in town, but he's at the enforcers' building and that he spent the night here without even calling me or letting me know he was okay. Have you been hiding him from me?"

Davis didn't want to fight with Nate. Nate was his mate's brother, and eventually, they would become a family.

He raised his hands. "I didn't keep Calvin from you. We

came back last night, and we were both exhausted. We just fell into bed." And they'd had sex, but Nate didn't need to know that.

Nate turned toward Calvin, who was hiding under the blankets, only his face exposed. His eyes widened when Nate looked at him, and suddenly, he was gone.

Davis knew Calvin hadn't told Nate he was a shifter yet, and he groaned because this was by far the worst way for Nate to find out.

"What the fuck?" Nate asked. He looked around. "Where did Calvin go? What happened to him?"

He turned toward Davis, who raised his hands. "Before you say anything, I had nothing to do with this. I didn't know Calvin was going to follow me until I found him in the hands of the Beasts."

Nate pointed toward the bed. "We're going to talk about that later, but right now, I want to know where he is. He was on the bed only seconds ago."

"He should have been the one to tell you this, but he's a shifter. He's still there. He just shifted."

Nate was silent for a second. Then he started yelling again. "What do you mean, my brother is a *shifter*? That's not possible. I'm human. He's human. He's always been human." He paused just the time to suck in a breath. "Did you turn him into a shifter? Is that what happened?"

Davis had had enough of being yelled at. He usually had enough patience to spare, but not today. He was still reeling from what had happened with the Beasts. He wanted a nice day with his mate, possibly in bed, but instead, he was being yelled at.

Nate was clearly in shock, and even though Davis understood why, he wasn't going to let anyone yell at him or Calvin.

"Calm the fuck down," he yelled back.

Nate jerked as if Davis had hit him. Davis stared at him until he finally nodded, then he turned around and headed to the bed. He lifted the blankets, and there Calvin was, in his bat form, looking up at him. Calvin's eyes were wide, but he didn't try to get away when Davis reached out and gently wrapped his fingers around him to lift him from the bed. He held him close to his chest, stroking his fur. "Everything is going to be okay," he crooned. He knew that the best way to get Calvin to shift back into his human form was to calm him down, and that was going to be hard enough as it was with Nate still in the room. "Whatever he says, whatever he does, you'll always have me. Got it?"

He waited until Calvin nodded to turn around and face Nate. "Sit down in the chair," he ordered. He might not be the leader of his team, but that didn't mean he couldn't lead when he needed to.

Nate stared at him for a second, then slowly obeyed. He didn't seem able to look away from the small bundle of fur and wings in Davis' hands, and Davis got it. He'd known Calvin as a shifter, but he could imagine were Nate was coming from and what he felt.

"Your brother is a shifter. You're going to have to accept that. And no, I didn't turn him into one. It doesn't work like that, and you know it," he told Nate.

Nate rubbed his face with both hands. "But how is that possible? He was human."

Davis shouldn't be the one to explain this, but he doubted Calvin would want to do it considering the situation. He looked down at his hands. "Can I tell him?"

He waited until Calvin nodded again to turn back to Nate. "It happened in the labs. Your brother was human when he was taken, but whatever they did to him, it changed him. He became a bat shifter. No one has ever taught him to control his shift or to fly, and he's had a hard time dealing with everything. You have to admit it was a lot, between the PTSD, the physical recovery, and this. That's one of the reasons he hid it from you."

Nate shook his head. "I don't understand."

"From what he told me, he was afraid to tell you. He wanted things to go back to the way they were before, but that can never happen. I think he was afraid that you would kick him out or refuse to talk to him if you found out he wasn't human anymore. You were so happy to have him back, and I know he was, too. He didn't want to ruin everything."

"But he wouldn't have ruined anything by telling me he was a shifter. For fuck's sake. Whatever he is, he's still my brother. I don't care if he can turn into a bat, a lion, or a cow. He's still Calvin, and all I've ever wanted was to have him back in my life. And I have that now. There's no way I'm ever pushing him away or giving him up unless he wants me out of his life. As long as he doesn't, I'm not going anywhere."

Nate turned his attention to Calvin, who was still in Davis' hands and didn't seem to want to leave. "I understand why you were so afraid. I don't know what I would do if I weren't human anymore. You have a lot of courage, much more than me. I'm so proud of you and everything you've done ever since you've come back. You're fighting tooth and nail to get your old life back, to get back to a normal life. And I understand that what I've been doing hasn't been helping. I didn't even think about it. I'm sorry I've been pushing you into something that wasn't possible. It wasn't what I was trying to do."

Davis stroked Calvin's fur again. He wanted Calvin to shift and talk to Nate. Davis might be able to talk him through the shift, but it was Calvin who would have to put the work into it.

Davis looked up at Nate. "I've been working with him over the past few weeks, so most of the time now, he can shift at will. But you surprised him, and he's scared. I can still feel his heart racing. He's going to need a few minutes to calm down."

"Of course. He can have all the time he needs. I don't even need him to shift right now. I do want to talk to him, but I get it. I can wait, even if it takes hours." Nate raked a hand through his hair. "And I'm sorry about the way I barged in and yelled at you. I was just worried. When Calvin disappeared without telling anyone what was happening, it was as if the past had caught up with me. I thought I'd lost him a second time, and I'm terrified that eventually, I'll lose him forever. He's my brother. I love him, and I want him to be happy. I know that whatever I feel doesn't have importance, but I don't want to lose him."

"And he doesn't want to lose you. He acted on instinct, and he was wrong. But all of that is in the past now. We're back, and we're not going anywhere."

Nate nodded. "Good. I don't know what I would do if I lost him again." His gaze drifted down to Davis' still naked chest. Davis knew Nate wasn't looking at him, but rather, at his brother. "I'm sorry. I hate that you were so afraid of me that you shifted. I'm not going to hurt you. I hope you know that." He rose from the chair. "I'm going to go home. Now that I know you're safe, it's not a problem. I'll stay there, and I'll still be there when you need me. If you want to talk to me, of course. You don't have to do anything you don't want to."

He moved toward the door, and Davis wondered if that was how things would end. Calvin and Nate needed to talk, and what better moment than now? But Calvin needed to shift for that to happen, and Davis wasn't sure he would be able to.

Calvin was terrified. He knew it was ridiculous, that he should swallow his fear and face his brother, but even after what Nate had said, he couldn't help it.

He and Nate had been trying so hard to go back to what they'd had before Calvin had been kidnapped, and now it was all ruined. Calvin would never be the same. He was a shifter, and there was no coming back from that.

But Nate didn't care. He'd just said so, and Calvin needed to believe him. He *did* believe him, even though the little voice in the back of his head was telling him that his best bet was to run. He refused to listen to that voice, though. He couldn't, not when he had everything he'd ever wanted — his brother, a mate, and soon, a home. He would do everything he could to get the life he'd always dreamed of, the life he thought about when he'd been in the labs.

He wiggled, silently trying to tell Davis to put him down. Davis looked at him, and a wave of affection flooded Calvin's chest. No matter what happened, he'd always have Davis. That much, he was sure of.

Davis loosened his hold, and Calvin climbed into his beard. It was kind of ridiculous, but he loved it. It made him feel safe, close to his mate, and he didn't want to face Nate right now.

"He can hear you," Davis told Nate.

"I know. I'm trying not to be offended by the fact that he's hiding, but it's hard."

"I realize that. But he loves you. He'd never want to disappoint you, and he thinks that by being a shifter, that's what he did.

"Which is ridiculous."

Calvin squeaked. He needed to stop hiding, no matter how safe he felt.

Calvin had to stop being afraid and to face his new reality. He'd been hiding ever since he'd been freed, but he had to start living his life.

He wiggled his way out of Davis' beard. Davis chuckled and helped him, because even though Calvin loved this, he still wasn't very good at using his bat body. It was going to take him a while to learn how to fly properly and how to move, but now, the thought wasn't as terrifying as it had been before. Even if Nate hadn't been accepting, Calvin would have still had people in his life, people who could help him. He and Davis had been working on controlling his shift when they'd been in the apartment, but the fear hadn't helped. Calvin had been hypervigilant, waiting for something to happen at any moment, and it had been hard to learn.

But things were different now. The Beasts were far away, and Calvin was home, or rather, as close to home as he could be. He doubted Davis would want to move in with Nate and Pryderi, so they would probably find a home somewhere else, but it would be here in Gillham.

Davis finally managed to untangle Calvin and gently put him on top of the bed. He sat next to him and stroked his fur, and Calvin shivered. It shouldn't be as arousing as it was considering he was in his bat form, but every time Davis touched him, he felt horny. Maybe it was the decade of not having sex. He felt like a teenager again, but anything that might happen with Davis would have to wait until Nate was on his way back home. For that to happen, Calvin needed to talk to his brother.

"Focus on your human form. Focus on what you do as a human, how you feel. You want to hug your brother, don't you?" Davis murmured.

Calvin nodded. He *did* want to do that. He wanted to tell Nate he was sorry. He wanted to tell him that he loved him, and that being a shifter hadn't changed anything. He was still the same Calvin—as much as he could be, with everything he'd been through.

"Good. Focus on him, then. You can do this. I know you can."

Calvin closed his eyes. It felt easier when he couldn't see

Nate and Davis staring at him expectantly. He took a deep breath, then another, and thought about how breathing felt when he was human. He thought about his arms, his legs, and before he knew it, he was human again. He felt the whisper of the sheet being pulled on top of his body, and he blinked his eyes open.

Davis and Nate were still looking at him, but their expressions were wildly different. Davis looked proud, while Nate was a little shocked.

Calvin swallowed and wrapped the sheet around his body. He wished he weren't naked to do this, and while he could ask Nate to step out so he could dress, he didn't want to make his brother wait. Nate had already waited enough. He'd no doubt been frantic when Calvin had left, and he deserved an explanation from Calvin.

Still, Calvin didn't want to do this naked. He rose from the bed and headed to the bathroom, but Nate was having none of that. He grabbed the edge of the sheet, and Calvin had to stop unless he wanted to be entirely naked in front of his brother — and he didn't. His naked body was for Davis' eyes only.

He swallowed and slowly turned to face Nate, making sure none of his body was visible. "I just want to put some clothes on," he explained.

"I know. I want you to put some clothes on, too. But I'm afraid that if we don't talk now, you're going to find a reason to avoid the conversation for weeks or even months. You've been avoiding it since you came back." Nate hesitated. "Because you already knew you were a shifter, didn't you? I mean, since you came back."

Calvin couldn't leave now. "Yeah. I've known since I became a shifter several years ago. I should have told you."

"But you were afraid I would hurt you. You were afraid I would reject you, that you would lose me and everything else."

"I know I shouldn't have been. It was stupid." Nate shook his head and pulled on the sheet until Calvin stepped closer. This was getting more awkward by the second, but Calvin went with it. "You're my brother," he continued. "You love me, and you always have."

"Damn right, I love you. That's never going to change."

"I shouldn't have doubted you."

"Don't you see? Fear isn't rational. You always knew that I loved you and that I wouldn't push you away, but you still felt like I would. That's not thinking. That's listening to your fears, and I get it. I understand why you would feel that way. I don't blame you."

"You're too good to me."

"I'm your big brother. I have to be." Nate smiled, and Calvin relaxed. He'd been afraid even after Davis had explained what was happening, but Nate was, well, Nate. He loved Calvin, and like he'd said, that wouldn't change.

"Come here," Nate said as he opened his arms.

He didn't have to repeat himself. Calvin stepped into the embrace, wrapping his arms around his brother and closing his eyes. He buried his face into Nate's shoulder and took a deep breath.

He didn't need to be afraid anymore. He was safe, and he had Nate. He had Davis.

He stepped away after what probably was too long a hug and realized he was still naked under the sheet. He gestured toward the bathroom. "Can I get dressed now?"

Nate chuckled. "Of course. I'll wait for you here unless you want me to go."

Calvin shook his head. "Stay, please." He looked at Davis. "Or do you have something planned?"

"Not as far as I know. I'll call Bran later and ask him what's going on, but I doubt he'll want to see us today. You can have time with your brother, don't worry."

"And with you. We're a family, right?"

"Of course we are."

Calvin couldn't help the smile that bloomed on his face. He suspected he was going to continue smiling for a while. He stepped toward the bathroom, but Nate cleared his throat. "By the way, I'll have a question for you once you leave the bathroom."

Calvin frowned. Maybe Nate wanted to talk about what kind of shifter he was? Calvin had never looked it up, to be honest. He knew he was a small bat, but that was where things stopped. He should probably be more curious, but until now, he'd hated that new side of himself. He'd been too worried, but it was part of him, an integral part he didn't want to push away anymore. "You can ask me whatever you want."

"Good. Because I was wondering how long you were going to ignore the fact that you and Davis are bonded."

Davis wasn't surprised that Nate had noticed the bite on both his and Calvin's necks. The man probably noticed a lot every day in the bar. It was part of his job.

Davis held his breath, wondering what Calvin was going to tell his brother. He couldn't deny he and Davis were bonded, because it was obvious, but he could explain *why* they'd bonded. He could tell Nate that it was only because they'd needed to, not because they'd wanted to. They couldn't change what they'd done, but the explanation *could* change things.

Calvin slapped a hand against his neck. "Shit."

Nate laughed. "I guess. Come on. Go to the bathroom, wash up, and get dressed. I'll still be here once you're done. I promise. You're going to have to work a lot harder if you want me to leave you alone."

Calvin shook his head. "I don't want you to go."

Before, he'd be in a rush to go to the bathroom, but now, he seemed hesitant, as if Nate might disappear during the time he was away. Davis took a step toward the brothers, kissed Calvin's cheek, and murmured, "Don't worry. I'll stay with him."

That seemed to do the trick. Calvin relaxed and headed to the bathroom. Davis waited until the door was closed behind him to turn toward Nate. "Thank you."

Nate blinked. "What for?"

"For not leaving. For giving Calvin the time he needed to deal with this."

"I hate that he thought I was going to abandon him. I've been looking for him for so long. I thought he was dead. Nothing is going to keep me away from him now that I know he's not. I have a second chance with him, and I'm not letting go."

"I think he knew that, but as you said, fear isn't rational. He let it guide his life until now, and I understand why. It can't have been easy for him to deal with everything that was done to him in the labs."

"You know he has nightmares."

Davis nodded. "I've been doing my best to help him, but I don't think I can do much."

"He's working with a therapist, but you're right. It won't be easy. It's probably going to take years for Calvin to feel more relaxed and for the fear to dissipate, but now he has you, and I feel better."

Davis frowned. "You do?" He'd thought that Nate would be angry, although maybe that wasn't fair. The one time Davis had met Nate as Calvin's mate had been weird. Calvin had still been hiding that he was a shifter, and Nate hadn't understood what was happening. He'd yelled at Davis, and Davis had eventually left. But this was different. Now Nate was aware of everything, and Davis hoped he would be accepting of their relationship.

Even if he wasn't, there was nothing he could do about it. No one could break a mate bond, not even the people who'd entered it. But Nate could make Davis' life difficult, and the last thing Davis wanted was for Calvin to have to choose between his mate and his brother.

Nate rubbed the back of his neck. "I apologize."

"What for?"

"For the way I treated you the day I found you with Calvin in your arms." He frowned. "What actually happened back then? Because Calvin never explained, and now that I know he's a shifter, I realize there's a lot more to it than I thought."

Davis laughed and picked up the t-shirt he'd left on the floor. He quickly put it on, his smile widening when he saw Nate look away. No matter how accepting Nate was, it had to be awkward for him to have the evidence right in front of him that his little brother had sex and was mated. "He'd shifted in the hallway," Davis explained.

Nate looked at him again. "At the bar?"

"Yeah. I went to the bathroom and saw him standing there. When I left, he was gone, but something was flying around, and not flying well, as you can imagine."

"You said no one taught Calvin to shift or fly."

"I don't think that the scientists in the lab wanted him to learn. It was good for them that he didn't know how to escape. Being so small could have helped him, but instead, he was at their mercy for so long. He's been trying to learn, but it's not easy, and since I'm a bear shifter, I can't do a lot for him. I don't know how to fly."

"But there are several bat shifters in the pack, right?"

"You're right, there are. I'm going to mention that to Calvin once he relaxes. I don't know if he's going to accept help from them or from anyone who isn't us, but I hope he will. He needs these people. He needs the pack." Every shifter should have a pack, a pride, a sleuth, or a group of people who were there for them and supported them.

"So once he shifted in the hallway, he wasn't able to get back to his human form, right?" Nate asked.

"Exactly. I didn't realize who he was in the beginning. He panicked and ended up tangled in my beard. It took me a while to untangle him, and when I did, I smelled him. I knew he was my mate, and I wanted to help him. He panicked when I mentioned you, so I took him to my car, and there, he was able to relax enough to shift back." Davis smiled at the memories. He'd never expected Calvin to be his mate. He'd stayed away from Calvin since Calvin had come back because he knew how hard life had been on him and how protective of him Nate was. Maybe he shouldn't have. He and Calvin would have had a lot more time together if he hadn't.

But he believed he and Calvin had met now for a reason. He didn't know what would have happened if they'd met sooner. He probably wouldn't have taken the job if he and Calvin had already been together. He wouldn't have wanted to spend too much time away from his mate. There was no way to know what would have happened to the pack then, and thinking about it wouldn't change anything.

"Thank you," Nate said. "You were there for him when I wasn't, and when he felt he couldn't trust me, and I'm grateful for that." He hesitated. "What happened when he went after you?"

Davis shook his head. "He knew I was going on a mission. I never expected him to follow me there. He wasn't in danger, though. I did everything I could to keep him safe, I promise."

"I have no idea what that mission was about, but I doubt that what you're saying is true. Whatever happened, it couldn't have been safe."

Davis shrugged. "You're right. It *was* dangerous. I was

undercover with the Beasts, trying to find out what they were planning for Gillham. I was stunned when Calvin arrived, but we made it work, and we both came home safe. He also was the one who found out what the Beasts are planning. I wouldn't be back here if it weren't for him."

Nate paled. "I don't like the sound of that, and I don't think I want any details."

"You don't need them. But I'm sure Calvin would tell you everything if you ever want to find out what happened."

"He's right," Calvin said as he came out of the bathroom. The ends of his hair were still damp, and he was wearing the same clothes he'd had on yesterday, but he looked good enough to eat, at least to Davis.

Davis wanted to drag him back to bed, but instead, he turned his attention back to Nate. He didn't know what was about to happen, but he suspected Nate didn't care that Calvin had bonded. He and Davis might not be best friends, but he was accepting, and Davis suspected that things would be okay for all of them.

Nate rose from the bed. "You put yourself in danger," he told Calvin.

"You're right. I did. But I don't regret it. I needed to get to Davis."

"I understand that. I would do everything possible to get to Pryderi if he was in that kind of danger. But you should have told me. Do you know how I felt when I couldn't find you? I thought you'd been taken again."

Calvin shuffled. "I know. I'm sorry. I should have thought better. I should have pushed for Bran to explain in more details." He snorted. "I should have thought, period. I panicked, though, and I went after my mate. But the past is the past. We should leave it behind and look to the future."

Calvin wasn't wrong, and Davis was ready to do just that.

Calvin didn't think he'd ever been so relieved, except maybe the day he'd finally been free from the Beasts and the labs.

Nate loved him. He was accepting him as he was, shifter and all. Calvin knew he'd have his brother's support when it came to learning how to shift and how to fly. Things might be awkward in the beginning, but eventually, everything would go back to normal.

Calvin had to believe it. He knew that the pack and the town were in danger, but his personal life was going great, and he couldn't help but hope that the same would go for everything else. Maybe he'd finally be lucky.

He'd spent so much time in the labs, so much time telling himself that this was how his life would go, how he would die, that he hadn't allowed himself to dream about what was next in the last few years of his captivity. He hadn't allowed himself to hope.

But he did now.

He stepped toward Nate and wrapped his arms around his brother. "Thank you, for everything."

Nate chuckled and hugged him back. "You don't have to thank me. You're my brother. I will always be here for you."

"I know. I've always known that. I should have trusted my instinct instead of freaking out."

"I'm not angry at you for doing it. I have no idea what you've been through, even though you've told me about it. I was never in your position, and I can only imagine. I don't blame you for being unsure and afraid. I love you. Just remember that, okay? Nothing else matters."

Calvin didn't want to cry, but he was close. His eyes prickled, and he rubbed his face when they stepped away. "What now?" he asked.

Nate smirked. "Well, I suppose I should leave the two of you alone. I've already taken enough of your time." He looked at the bed, and Calvin knew it was obvious that Calvin and Davis had been up to something more than sleeping. "You two are newly mated, and I remember all too well how that goes."

Calvin blushed and punched his brother's shoulder. "You're still newly mated, too. It's not like you and Pryderi have been together long."

"You're right, and he's waiting for me at home. He was worried, and so was Yedley."

Shit. Calvin hadn't thought about that. He hadn't thought about anything except Davis and finding him when he'd left, and he should have.

He'd thought he was alone. He'd been alone for so long, and it was hard for him to remember that he had other people to think about now. But he did. He needed to think about Nate, about Pryderi. He had Yedley and Justin, and possibly the rest of Davis' team. He was only close to his immediate family, but that would change. He was Davis' mate, and where Davis went, his team did, too. Calvin was going to have to get used to that.

But before he did, he needed to text Yedley and tell him he was okay. Yedley was going to kick his ass, but he deserved it. He deserved all the yelling he was going to get.

He shouldn't be as happy as he was about it, but he couldn't help it. "I'll text Yedley and tell him we'll talk later. And please, tell Pryderi I'm fine. And that I'm sorry, of course. I never meant to make any of you worry."

Nate patted Calvin's shoulder. "I know. But you did, and you need to start thinking like you have a family, because you do. You're not alone anymore. You're never going to be alone again."

That should probably scare Calvin, but he couldn't bring himself to feel anything but happy about it.

He and Calvin walked Nate downstairs so he could leave.

It was the first look Calvin had gotten at the house, and he wasn't surprised to find it busy. People were around, watching TV in the living room, cooking in the kitchen, exercising in the gym. Calvin knew this was Davis' home, at least for now, but he wished they were alone. He didn't like having this many people around. It brought back memories of the lab, where there was always someone around. Calvin had never been alone there, but now he was, or at least, he had been when he'd been at Nate's. He'd spent so much time on his own in his bedroom that now he had to get used to being around people again.

He'd made a mistake there, too, but it didn't matter. He had time, or at least, he hoped he would. All of that would depend on what the Beasts did and how the pack defended itself.

He waved at Nate as Nate drove away and leaned against Davis, wrapping an arm around his waist. Davis kissed Calvin's temple, and even though Calvin grumbled, he was starting to love those kisses, the gentle, caring touches.

"That went well, didn't it?" Davis asked.

Calvin couldn't deny it had. "Way better than I thought."

"I know how hard it can be, but you have to ignore those negative feelings that tell you that you're going to end up alone. You're not. You'll always have someone who loves you around, be it me, Nate, or someone else. You have more people than you think."

Calvin was starting to realize that. "I know."

Davis kissed him again. "Why don't we go have breakfast? I'm sure you're hungry, and even if you're not, I certainly am."

Calvin laughed. "Sure. Let's go." He might as well start spending more time around the people that were a part of Davis' team, and that meant they were going to be part of Calvin's life, too.

His life. It was far from being perfect, and it was nothing like what he'd imagined when he was a teenager or a young adult, but considering what had happened to him and where he'd been a few months ago, it was heaven on earth.

Breakfast was busy and noisy. Calvin focused on his food, though, and it made it easier to deal with. He was grateful that no one tried talking to him. There were other enforcers in the kitchen, and several of them stopped to say hello to Davis or talk to him, but no one even gave Calvin a second glance. They treated him as if he were one of them, even though he wasn't.

That was what family was like, wasn't it? Even before Calvin had been taken, he'd only had Nate. Their parents had died when Calvin was a teenager, and Nate had taken care of him. Even when their parents had been alive, there was only the four of them. Calvin wasn't used to having a lot of people, and he didn't know how to deal with it.

But he would learn, for Davis.

Calvin didn't know what would happen. He didn't know if the pack would be safe, but he prayed it would. He wanted to make it his home. It already was, even though he hadn't meant for it to happen. In the weeks since he'd been back — even though he'd stuck to his bedroom and the bar — he'd become part of Gillham. He'd become part of the pack, and that wasn't going to change. He wouldn't let it. Things were perfect for now. They were perfect for *Calvin*.

And it was enough.

CHAPTER SEVEN

"Thanks to Davis and his mate, we now have a list of names of people who are planning to attack the pack," Bran said.

The team turned to look at Davis, and he wiggled his fingers at them. That got him a few chuckles and a few eye rolls, but he didn't care. He was back with his team, where he belonged.

"What's going to happen to those people?" Justin asked.

"Well, we're still checking the names, just in case. We need to be aware of why they're doing this. Some of them might be helping the Beasts because they're being blackmailed into it, or for other reasons."

"And once you know they're doing it because they're assholes?"

There were more chuckles in the room, and Davis relaxed.

It was weird to come back to work after spending so much time alone with Calvin. Even when he'd been with the Beasts, he'd spent as little time with them as possible, just enough to get information. And still, Calvin had been the one who'd found out about everything.

Once they'd come back, Davis and Calvin had spent a few days in Davis' bedroom. Davis knew that wouldn't last forever. Calvin wanted to go home, and the two of them needed to start looking for a house. There was no way they could live in the enforcers' building, no matter how much Davis loved his team. He liked most of the enforcers, but they were noisy, and there were a lot of them. He wanted Calvin to have a home, a safe haven, and it wasn't Davis' room in the enforc-ers' building.

"Someone will look into it. You don't have to worry about that," Bran said.

Davis wrinkled his nose. He hadn't expected Bran to tell them that they'd be the ones in charge. The enforcers were not professional killers. They hadn't been created for that. Davis wouldn't have had a problem going after those people, and he knew that if there had been more time, the council would have wanted them to be arrested rather than killed. But they couldn't risk it.

"Who's going to take care of them? The enforcers?" Lorcan asked.

Bran shook his head. "That's not for you to worry about."

"It's our job."

"No, it's not. There's no time to investigate these people and find a reason to arrest them. I wish there was. I like the idea as little as you do. We shouldn't kill people. We're not judge and jury. But this is how things need to go. The safety of the pack and the town are the most important thing. Eve-rything else comes after that. I know some of you won't like it, and you're free to have your own opinion, or even to leave the enforcers if that's what you want."

Davis wasn't about to do that yet. He needed to talk to Cal-vin about what their future would be like, but for now, he wasn't leaving the enforcers. He loved his job—undercover missions notwithstanding—and as long as he could stay here and have his own house with Calvin, he wasn't going to quit. He knew he'd be more careful from now on because he had someone to come back to once his missions were over, but a lot of enforcers dealt with that. They had mates, a family, and that didn't mean they quit their job.

Davis wasn't going to, either, not for a while.

"Any more questions?" Bran asked. His expression was

uncompromising, and Davis understood.

Bran wasn't wrong when he said that some people weren't going to like this. If Davis was honest with himself, *he* didn't like it. He didn't want people to die. He didn't want to become a killer, even though he would gladly do it if it meant keeping Calvin and the town safe.

He was relieved he wouldn't have to, though. He suspected that the enforcers weren't the only team the council had at their disposal to do that kind of thing. He'd been present when another team had been called in, and no explanation had been given. Those people had moved like they knew what they were doing. Davis might not know who they were, but he suspected that the council had a small team of professional killers who took care of the jobs no one else wanted.

He could deal with that. As long as he didn't have blood on his hands and the people that he cared for were safe, it would be okay.

"Thank you," Sue said as she rose from her chair. She looked at her team. "If you have any more questions or doubts, you're welcome to come to me, of course. But you heard everything Bran had to say, and I don't have any more information."

Davis got up and stretched. The team disbanded, and he was eager to go back to Calvin. For now, the team wasn't going anywhere. All the enforcers' teams had been ordered to stay in Gillham, just in case Bates and Elroy realized what had happened and decided to attack even though they didn't have the numbers yet. Davis hoped that wouldn't happen, but just like every other enforcer, he was hypervigilant, and that wouldn't stop until they knew that the danger had passed.

"Justin? Can I ask you a question?" Lorcan asked, sidling closer to Justin.

Davis frowned. He still needed to talk to his best friend. He hadn't found the time yet since he'd mostly been spending his free time with Calvin. That needed to change, though. Both Davis and Calvin had friends, family, other people they needed to focus on. No matter how much Davis wished he and Calvin could be their own island and not care about anything but their relationship, that wasn't the case.

"Of course. What's going on?" Justin asked as the three of them left the room where they'd had the meeting.

Neither of them had asked Davis to stick with them, but Davis was planning to talk to Lorcan as soon as Justin was gone.

"I just wanted to ask you about Devon. Is he okay?"

Justin blinked, and Davis shared his confusion. "Devon?"

"You know. I was wondering if he was okay after what happened."

"He's doing okay, yes. Why do you ask?"

Lorcan shrugged and pushed his hands into his pockets. "Nothing. Just wondering."

"Are you sure? Because we all noticed how weird you were with him," Davis pointed out.

Lorcan scowled at him, but Davis didn't care. The team was a family, and even if Lorcan didn't want all of them to know what was going on, he should at least tell Davis. They were best friends.

What was happening that Lorcan didn't want to share with Davis?

"I'd like to see him if that's okay," Lorcan said as he turned his attention back to Justin.

Justin frowned. "I can certainly ask him if he's willing to talk to you, but I'm not sure his answer will be yes. Can you tell me what's going on?"

Lorcan shook his head. "Never mind that. I just wanted to know if he was okay."

Justin stopped in the middle of the hallway and crossed his arms over his chest. "If he wants to talk to you, I'll let you know. But he's a friend. He lives with Yedley and me. I trust you, but I'd still like to know what's going on before I talk to him about this."

Lorcan hesitated, and Davis held his breath. He hated that Lorcan didn't feel comfortable enough to talk to Davis. He couldn't even begin to imagine what was going on. As far as he knew, Lorcan had always told him everything.

Lorcan sighed, and his shoulders slumped. "He's my mate."

Davis blinked. He wasn't sure what he'd been expecting, but it wasn't that. "You're sure?" he asked.

Lorcan nodded. "Yeah. I was sure as soon as I smelled him."

"And you haven't told him," Justin said. It wasn't a question, but Lorcan answered anyway.

"I haven't. I don't know what to do about it. I want to tell him, but after finding out what his last relationship was like, I'm pretty sure it would send him running for the hills screaming bloody murder. I don't think I can deal with that."

Justin patted Lorcan's shoulder. "I can't tell you what to do, of course. And I *will* talk to Devon and ask him if he wants to talk to you, if that's what you want. But maybe you should tell him. Being mates is different from being boyfriends, and even though I'm sure you're right and that he's not looking forward to his next relationship, he should still know about this. It wouldn't be fair to keep it from him."

Davis agreed with Justin, but he wasn't sure Lorcan would take that suggestion. He wished he could do more for his best friend. He wanted Lorcan to have what he had with Calvin, and he wasn't sure that could happen. Devon didn't trust anyone, and it would take a lot of work for that to change.

Davis leaned closer to Lorcan. "You need to give him time."

Lorcan rubbed his face. "I know. I've been trying to."

"Have faith in your bond and in yourself. If there's anyone who can show Devon a relationship doesn't have to be hell, it's you. After what happened with Calvin, I truly believe that mates meet at a certain moment for a reason. Devon needs you, even though he doesn't realize that yet. I'm sure you'll do the right thing." And Davis would be there every step of the way to support Lorcan and Devon if they needed him.

He had his happy ever after, and he wanted his best friend to have one, too.

You may also enjoy the following from eXtasy Books Inc:

Hopping to Happiness
Catherine Lievens

Excerpt

Bryce peeked around the dumpster, and once he was sure no one was in the alley, he hopped out. He sniffed, but the only thing he could smell was trash. It stank, and he wrinkled his nose.

He'd thought that hiding behind the restaurant would help him find food, but from the looks of it, he was going to have to shift. He didn't want to. He was vulnerable as a rabbit, but it would be even worse as a naked human. God knew what people would think of him if they saw him. Probably that he was a pervert, walking around naked in the hopes of finding someone.

That wouldn't do. He might be hungry, but he wasn't about to become a sex offender because of that. Maybe he could wait until it was dark to shift and go through the trash. He wasn't sure he would find something he could eat, but it was better than not looking at all. He was hungry. He needed food. Besides, in his rabbit form, he could survive on vegetables. It wouldn't be good for long, but for a while, it would be enough.

He sighed and went back under the dumpster. He wished he could still be home right now. He wanted to go back, but that would only happen if he told his alpha that he wasn't gay, maybe that he'd seen the light.

Bryce snorted. Seen the light. Right. Because that was how things worked. He knew damn well it wasn't, but he supposed he could fool his alpha if he tried. The fact was that he didn't want to, though.

Bryce was gay. Very gay. He'd only ever gotten hard for guys, and that wasn't going to change anytime soon. He should have known better than trying to date, though. He should have known better than to think that his alpha would be accepting. He'd been riding on the high that his own family didn't care when he'd decided to come out publicly.

It hadn't gone well.

Bryce's family might not care about who he fucked, but his alpha certainly did. He'd given Bryce an ultimatum — either Bryce became straight and married a woman, or he got kicked out of the nest.

And kicked out Bryce had been.

He wasn't even angry at his family for not standing up for him. He understood. They needed the support the nest could give them, the work, the money, the food. It was hard to be a shifter out here, especially with humans not knowing about them. They had to hide if they wanted to be their true selves, and humans didn't usually understand why they lived all together. They thought they were cults, and while that wasn't true, it certainly felt like it right now.

It was because of the nest that Bryce wouldn't have his family anymore. It was because of the nest, or rather, of the alpha, that Bryce was homeless and going through the trash to eat.

He sighed, then sneezed because of the stink. Dammit. He needed to stop thinking about what he'd left behind. He'd made his choice. It wasn't going to change, no matter how much he wished it would. He wasn't ever going to become straight, so this was his life now.

Bryce knew he would make it, eventually. He was a good person. He would find work and earn enough to get an apartment. It was these first few steps that were the hardest, and his stomach didn't like being empty. He supposed he should be grateful. Maybe like this, he would finally lose a few pounds. Alpha Johnson had always told him he could use it.

He stuck his head out from under the dumpster again and looked around. Staying here wasn't useful. Even if he waited until later to go through the trash, the evening was still a few hours away. The days were slowly becoming longer as spring advanced, so he would have to be careful.

But there was a park nearby. Bryce didn't like eating grass—it made him feel too much like a cow, which he definitely wasn't, even though he'd always been overweight—but it would do in a pinch since he was so hungry. And bonus—grass didn't have a lot of calories.

He hopped out, moving slowly to be sure no one would notice him. He didn't think people would care if they found a rabbit hopping around, but you never knew. Someone might take pity on him and take him home, which would be a good thing if he could be sure of what would happen to him once he got there. He'd heard enough horror stories, though. It was the kind of stuff shifter parents told her kids at night so they'd be careful around humans, and since Bryce didn't fancy becoming rabbit stew, he was going to stick to what he knew and stay away from people.

He made it to the park. He wasn't sure how much time had passed, and he didn't care. He was a rabbit. Time was of no consequence for him.

He hid under a bush and started munching on grass, wrinkling his nose at the taste. He didn't like it, but his stomach was grumbling, and he needed to fill it. Maybe Alpha Johnson had been right. Maybe Bryce should have been a cow shifter.

Bryce shook his head. No. He needed to stop thinking

about the alpha. The man had kicked him out for something Bryce couldn't change and didn't want to change. Bryce was gay, and he was proud of it. Well, he supposed he should say that he was proud of it as much as anyone could be proud of their sexuality. It wasn't like straight people went around saying they were proud of liking the other sex. But Bryce had never thought this was a problem for him. It didn't feel like it was. He didn't feel weird or unnatural. He felt like Bryce, and that was it. He didn't want to change only because some people thought he was wrong. Besides, if it wasn't the gay thing, it would be something else. Alpha Johnson had always had a problem with Bryce. In the beginning, it was just that Bryce was fat. Now, it was this. That was never going to change, and Bryce had had enough.

Still, he should probably have waited to come out until he had money set aside. Instead, he found himself in the middle of the street, with not even a pair of jeans to call his own. Luckily for him, it was spring, but still, the nights were cold.

"Look at how pretty you are," a voice cooed.

Bryce froze. He slowly turned his head and found a lady standing over him. He tried to hop away, but she was fast, somehow faster than he was. She snatched him from the ground and raised him to her chest, and Bryce tried to bite her.

He didn't want to become rabbit stew, dammit.

"Oh, no, you don't. I know you don't want to come with me, but I promise everything will be okay. I'm going to give you food, and you'll be warm and safe."

Bryce wrinkled his nose. Was she telling the truth? She wouldn't have a reason to lie to him since she didn't know he was a shifter, but could he trust her? He supposed that no one would tell a rabbit they were planning to eat that he was about to become stew, but still.

He kicked, trying to push his way out of her arms, but even though she was elderly, she was damn strong. She didn't let go, instead walking away from the park and toward a car.

Bryce knew there was no way he would make it out if he got into that car, but he didn't have a say in it. He was just a rabbit shifter. Even if he bit her, she probably wouldn't let him go. She'd decided she needed to save him, and that was what she was going to do.

His eyes widened when she opened the back of the car and he saw a box inside. She gently put him inside, and he tried to hop out, but she was already closing the box.

This wasn't good. This wasn't good at all.

Bryce had no idea what was happening when the car started to move. He didn't know where he was going or what was going to happen to him. It was terrifying, and he didn't know what to do about it. No matter how hard he tried to push the box sideways, it wasn't budging, and neither was he.

He had no idea how long it had been when the car finally stopped. He held his breath, listening to the sounds of the lady turning the car off, stepping out, and walking around to get him. He was ready to fight as soon as he was out of the box, but of course, instead of taking him out, the lady picked up the entire box and walked away with it.

Great. Bryce was sure he'd make for a damn fine rabbit stew, but he still hoped she'd choke on it.

About the Author

Catherine is the creator of several series, most of them paranormal, including the Whitedell Pride Series and the Gillham Pack Series. While she graduated in translation, she decided to go the writer's way because it was more fun to create her own stories and characters.

She's been living in Italy for more than twenty years, but she's a daughter of the North—Belgium to be precise—and she misses it so much that she's already planning to move back.

She loves pizza—probably too much—her son, her pets, and of course, books. She sneaks some reading time into her schedule every time she has five minutes free from writing, demands from her various pets and son, and lastly, housework.

Connect with her:

lievens.catherine@gmail.com
BookBub: https://www.bookbub.com/authors/catherine-lievens

Website: https://authorcatherinelievens.wordpress.com/

Facebook: https://www.facebook.com/catherine.lievens.9
Facebook Group: https://www.facebook.com/groups/411788002341528/

Twitter: https://twitter.com/authorCLievens
Newsletter: http://eepurl.com/c-uvKn

www.ingramcontent.com/pod-product-compliance
Lightning Source LLC
Chambersburg PA
CBHW060618130626
46555CB00002B/552